T0193506

SABRINA BANNER

THE SOUL OF A SORCERER

ISABEL SKOWFOE

authorHOUSE®

AuthorHouse™
1663 Liberty Drive
Bloomington, IN 47403
www.authorhouse.com
Phone: 1 (800) 839-8640

This is a work of fiction. All of the characters, names, incidents, organizations, and dialogue
in this novel are either the products of the author's imagination or are used fictitiously.

Published by AuthorHouse 06/22/2018

ISBN: 978-1-5462-4828-6 (sc)
ISBN: 978-1-5462-4827-9 (e)

Library of Congress Control Number: 2018907442

Print information available on the last page.

Any people depicted in stock imagery provided by Getty Images are models,
and such images are being used for illustrative purposes only.
Certain stock imagery © Getty Images.

This book is printed on acid-free paper.

This book is dedicated to my best friend, Ania Keidong, and my dad for helping me make this book into what it is today. Ania, thank you for helping me with creating this new, magical world, and thanks for your help with the plot and creating the character Aureum Cor. Dad, thank you for being patient and having faith in my writing while I wrote the book, and for helping me get it published.

Contents

Author's Note

Dear Readers,

This book would not be possible without the following people in my life. I would like to take a second to thank my ninth and tenth grade English teachers, Jonathan Bright and Marissa Lombardo, respectively, for helping me improve writing, as well as my sixth grade science teacher, Linda Reed, for introducing me to Percy Jackson, which was the beginning of my love for books.

I'd also like to thank my mom and Great Grandma Lillian Cooper. My mom helped me keep my head on straight and was there when I needed her. My great grandma was such a remarkable woman. She passed away early in 2018, but she was a very important person in my life.

The journey for this book to become what it is now has taken roughly three years, and I couldn't be happier with the outcome. I hope that you enjoy this book and love these characters as much as I do.

Sincerely,
Isabel Skowfoe

Summary

Fifteen-year-old Sabrina Banner thought that she had her life figured out. But she was proven wrong when a man named Sylvester Coulson appeared on her doorsteps at three o'clock in the morning. Sabrina's normal life suddenly took an unexpected twist, and she found herself tossed into a world of magic with an unavoidable, prewritten prophecy deciding her fate.

Author's Biography

Most kids don't know what they want to be when they group up, but fifteen-year-old Isabel Skowfoe has known from the start. She has always had a passion for writing, and since she was little, she has aspired to become an author. Isabel can often be found writing or reading, working on ways to improve her love for storytelling. Isabel was born on May 23, 2002, and shortly after birth, she was diagnosed with DiGeorge/22q.11.2. DiGeorge is a rare syndrome that results in the deletion of a section of chromosome number 22. Isabel has an older sibling and a younger sibling. Apart from writing, Isabel enjoys drawing, theater, film, and photography, and she has a major love for everything Marvel, Star Wars, and Disney. In the words of her family, she is a walking and talking Disney encyclopedia. Isabel hopes to share her stories with those around her and continue to do what she loves.

I. "A Restless Night"

For Sabrina Banner's whole life, she believed herself to be nothing but ordinary. She felt as though she had been cheated and born in the wrong world or in the wrong time, where everything had already been discovered. There was not a single thing that was odd about her. But it wasn't her fault that she was born in a loving household, in a world where magic and adventure didn't exist. Aside for wishing for things to be slightly more interesting, at this point in time, Sabrina's life was going well. But we all know that nothing good lasts forever.

"Good morning, Sabrina!" Paris Clark greeted her younger cousin with a bright smile and a mouthful of food, with milk dribbling down her chin.

Sabrina yawned tiredly but managed to force a smile. "Hi, Paris. You, um, you got a little something …" Sabrina pointed to the side of her face in an attempt to mimic the milk that was dripping from Paris's chin.

Paris didn't seem to take the hint as she cocked her head in confusion. "I got a little …?"

Sabrina sighed and shook her head. "Never mind. It's nothing." She placed her backpack down by the doormat, and then she made herself some toast and spread some raspberry jam over it. After that, Sabrina joined Paris at the table and nibbled on her toast.

"Good morning, girls!" Aunt Jeanette's voice rang out as she entered the room.

"Hey, Mom," Paris said with a smile.

"Hi, Aunt Jen," Sabrina greeted.

Aunt Jeanette smiled as she planted a small kiss on both of their heads and grabbed a water bottle from the fridge. "You two had better hurry up and head off to school, or you'll be late. I've gotta get down to the bakery. Kenzie said she'd be there early this morning, so I could rest, but I can't leave her to do everything. What kind of boss would I be if I did that?" Aunt Jeanette laughs.

That was one of the big things that Sabrina loved about Aunt Jeanette: she was so caring and always put others before herself. She was always ready to assist anyone in need, and she was supportive of everything. Whenever Sabrina felt down, she'd go to Aunt Jeanette, who would know exactly how to cheer up Sabrina. She was a perfect pretend mother for Sabrina, considering that Sabrina had lost her mom when she was younger.

"I'll see you girls later. You and your friends are meeting at the bakery after school, right, Sabrina?" Aunt Jeanette asked as she grabbed her keys off of the hook and slid on her shoes.

Sabrina nodded and swallowed a piece of toast before answering, "That's the plan, anyway."

"Well, if the plan changes, give me a call, all right?" Aunt Jeanette said, and Sabrina nodded again. "Good. Have a great day at school, you two." Aunt Jeanette beamed as she opened the door.

"Have a great day at work, Mom!" Paris echoed brightly.

"Oh! It's cold out!" Aunt Jeanette shivered as the cold wind blew inside. She zipped up her jacket and put some thin gloves on her hands. "Don't forget gloves and a hat. I know that spring break is tomorrow but it's still cold out and I don't want sick kids when I come home."

Sabrina smiled. "Sure thing, Aunt Jeanette."

Aunt Jeanette waved to Paris and Sabrina before exiting the house and leaving them on their own.

"Finish up, Sabrina, unless you plan on taking the bus. I will leave without you," Paris warned as she got up to put her bowl in the sink.

Sabrina's eyes get big in horror. "I'm going, I'm going! Don't rush me!"

Sabrina quickly stuffed the last of her toast into her mouth. Paris wasn't bluffing—Sabrina knew that for a fact. Paris had deliberately left Sabrina behind before, and Sabrina had to ride the smelly, loud school bus for fifteen minutes. After that, Sabrina had learned quickly that Paris was a person of her word.

"*Meow.*"

Sabrina cringed and glanced down from the stool she was sitting on to find Paris's big, orange, fat cat, Suki, who was gazing up at her with her big, rust-colored eyes. Sabrina groaned and yelled, "Paris, did you feed the cat yet?"

"Oh, shoot! I forgot! Sabrina, can you do it, please? I need to start up the car," Paris said with a sheepish smile as she grabbed her car keys and backpack.

"Do I have a choice in this?"

"Nope!" Paris's voice rang out in a song—like way.

Sabrina let out a huff in annoyance as she begrudgingly got up from her seat. "Yeah, that's what I figured," she grumbled as she carefully avoided stepping on Suki's oversized body. Suki still glared at her anyway.

Sabrina sucked in her breath as she scurried over to the pantry, found the cat food, and brought it over to Suki's dish. Sabrina quickly poured Suki's dry cat food as Suki dashed over to eat it. When Suki reached the dish, she hissed at Sabrina and scratched Sabrina's hand before Sabrina could pull it out of Suki's reach. Sabrina yelped in pain and yanked away her hand. Sabrina wanted to curse, but she bit her lip to keep herself from doing so. Aunt Jeanette hated cursing and using "colorful language." Sabrina would normally never swear aloud, but she often did in her head.

In fact, if the girls did swore aloud and were heard by Aunt Jeanette, they had to put ten bucks in a swear jar. The clear jar sat on the windowsill by the sink, and Sabrina hated it. She'd accidentally let a few swear words slip before and had been forced to give up ten bucks. Not fun.

Ignoring her wandering thoughts, Sabrina quickly put a bandage around her scratched thumb and grumpily slung her backpack over one shoulder.

Paris had already headed out the door to start the car, and Sabrina could only pray to the gods that Paris hadn't left without her.

Sabrina rushed over to close the door behind her and locked it before dashing to the front of the driveway, where Paris had fortunately waited for Sabrina in her little red car. Paris honked the horn at Sabrina and yelled, "Come on, Sabrina! School starts soon. Hurry up!"

Sabrina dashed toward Paris's car, and plopped down in the passenger's side putting her backpack on her lap. "Sorry … that I'm … late …" Sabrina panted between breaths as Paris rolled out of the driveway. "Suki … hates me."

"Suki hates you? That's no surprise. She's always seemed to hate you. She's such a great cat, and loves Aunt Jeanette and me. I wonder what you possibly could've done to make her hate you?"

Sabrina decided to be smart and play dumb. "I have no idea. Guess I'm just not a cat magnet like you and Aunt Jeanette." Paris nodded, and the rest of the ride was in silence. Suki and Sabrina had never been on good grounds from the moment they adopted her.

Sabrina thought back to the times when she had tried to give away Suki, ship Suki to China, and lock her in a closet. Sure, Sabrina hadn't always been the nicest to the oversized feline, but Suki had her moments as well. Suki had scratched Sabrina multiple times, hissed at her, and clawed her legs, so in Sabrina's defense she wasn't the only one at fault.

Sabrina realized that she and Paris were almost to school, and she decided that she needed to stop arguing with her internal dialogue.

The next thing Sabrina knew, Paris had pulled into a parking lot with ten minutes to spare before the homeroom bell rang. The two of them got out of the car and went their separate ways to their lockers to begin their last day of school before spring break.

Fortunately for Sabrina, the school day had finally come to an end.

She tiredly sat down in the passenger seat next to Paris, while her best friends, Jason Sullivan and Demi O'Hara, hopped in the backseat. "I wonder what Mrs. Clark's special is today at her bakery?" Demi remarked pensively.

"I think she told me that it was chocolate chip muffins last night." Paris answered as she kept her eyes glued to the road.

"Yum!" Jason exclaimed, excitement evident in his eyes.

Because Sabrina was sitting in the passenger seat, she stole a quick a glance at her best friends from the rear-view mirror to see Jason licking his lips and Demi rolling eyes.

Demi playfully shoved Jason. "Grow up, Jase! Honestly. They're just muffins!"

Jason gasped in pretend horror. "Just muffins? How dare you! Muffins are amazing, *Demetria!*" Jason scolded Demi with a disappointed head shake. Sabrina rolled her eyes in exasperation, but a small smile of amusement played on her lips.

"You two are so immature," Sabrina noted with a giggle.

"First of all, Jason, do not call me Demetria! Second, I am not immature! It's Jason who's the immature one!" Demi whined.

Sabrina sighed. "And that, my dear friend, proves my point. I rest my case."

"Can we just say that you're all immature and call it a day?" Paris interjected, stifling a laugh with a smirk on her lips.

Sabrina heard a few muffled mumbles of protest from Jason and Demi, but nothing other than that. After letting out a deep breath, Sabrina leaned back in her seat, preparing herself for the rest of the ride.

It was sometime after nine o'clock when Sabrina and her friends left the bakery. Just as Paris had said, chocolate chip muffins had been the special that night, and Jason couldn't have been happier. After the muffins, Paris had dropped Jason and Demi off at their houses before heading home for the night. Aunt Jeanette had driven home separately, insisting that she needed to stay and prepare for the next day.

When Sabrina and Paris got home, Paris fed Suki again, and then the two went to their separate bedrooms. Sabrina slipped on some warm pajamas, turned off her light, and snuggled into her bed, ready for sleep to take over. Eventually after counting sheep for what felt like forever and staring mindlessly up at her ceiling, Sabrina's eyelids grew heavy, and she found herself entering the Realm of Morpheus.

"Sea! Sea, wake up! Sabrina!" A panicked voice chided.

Sabrina groaned and tiredly mumbled, "No, let me sleep ..."

"Sabrina, don't make me drag you out of bed! Get up!"

A sigh escaped Sabrina's lips as she slowly pushed herself up into a sitting position. Her vision was slightly blurry from just waking up, and so she waited a second for it to focus. "Sabrina, come on!" Sabrina's hearing finally kicked in, and she recognized the voice as belonging to her older cousin, Paris.

"Paris, let me—ah!" Sabrina cried as Paris roughly grabbed Sabrina's arm, tugged her out of her warm bed, and yanked her up to her feet.

"It's urgent!" Paris exclaims.

Sabrina exhaled deeply in exasperation and rubbed her eyes again in an attempt to wake herself up more as Paris practically dragged her out of her bedroom and towards the living room.

"Paris, it's three in the morning. What could be so important that you had to yank me out of my bed and bring me into the…" Sabrina started, but she suddenly stopped dead in her tracks.

She tilted head in confusion when she saw Aunt Jeanette talking to a man with long, shaggy, pepper-colored hair that reached slightly past his shoulders. Sabrina wriggled her wrist from Paris's grasp and took a cautious step forward.

"Ah, Miss Sabrina Annalise Banner!" The man at the door beamed with outstretched arms as he turned his attention from Aunt Jeanette to Sabrina.

Sabrina frowned and looked at him suspiciously. "Do I know you? How do you know my name?" she asked.

"Oh, how rude of me! Allow me to introduce myself." The man smiled, and his dusty blue eyes twinkled. "My name is Sylvester. Do I have a last name? Of course I do. But I hate using it, so, just Sylvester please." The stranger smiled.

"Okay … But how do you know *my* name? I've never met or seen you before. *Ever.*" Sabrina noted.

Sylvester chuckled softly. "I've always been around, Miss Sabrina. I'm always watching you, looking out for you. Just as I promised your father I would," he said with a hint of sadness in his voice.

"My … my father?" Sabrina repeated.

"Yes. Frederick Banner. My best friend, and the father that you've never met. I owe everything to him."

"You knew my Dad? You're his best friend? But—but how?" Question upon question piled up in Sabrina's head, which made her feel a little lightheaded from the sudden overwhelming feeling.

Aunt Jeanette placed a hand of comfort on Sabrina's shoulder. "Sabrina, your father wasn't … normal," she began, choosing her words slowly.

Sylvester laughed slightly. "Not normal? Of course he wasn't normal!

No one's normal. That being said, your father was even more abnormal than most of you petty mortals."

Aunt Jeanette glared at him. "Don't you dare call Paris and me that! Just because you were born in a different realm, with different rules, that doesn't mean that you can look down on the Mortal Realm. It's absurd!"

Sabrina flinched slightly at her aunt's sharp tone.

Sabrina had rarely heard her raise her voice before. Aunt Jeanette was normally such a happy and calm person. Even when she was angry, she was good at holding it in. Many people referred to her as the Peacekeeper.

"Relax, Jeanette. I'm only speaking the truth. But we don't have time to fuss over little things like this." Sylvester waved his hand as if dismissing the subject.

"Fine, we'll put a pin in this. But the argument is not over!" Aunt Jeanette fumed with her nose raised in the air.

Sylvester laughed. "Put a pin in it? *Hilarious!* You mortals never really change, do you?"

Paris and Sabrina shared a look, and it seemed as though Paris was just as confused as Sabrina. "Um, can you please stop beating around the bush and get to the point!" Sabrina blurted in annoyance, losing any patience that she had left.

Aunt Jeanette had her mouth open, ready to argue with Sylvester again, but she quickly composed herself and nodded stiffly. "Yes, of course. I'm sorry, Sabrina. Paris, Sabrina, please go and sit on the couch and make sure that he doesn't touch anything until I get back."

Aunt Jeanette glared at Sylvester before wandering out of the room.

Sabrina glanced at Sylvester, who was absentmindedly playing with the leaf of a plant that sat beside the door in a red vase. Sighing, Paris and Sabrina shared a look again, and Paris shrugged sheepishly, not knowing what to do.

After awkwardly clearing her throat, Sabrina said, "I guess we should … go to the living room?"

Although it came out sounding more like a question, Paris nodded. "Lead the way, Sea." Paris beckoned, and Sabrina gave Paris a quizzical glance.

"This is your house too, Paris," Sabrina noted before she made her way to the white couch in the center of the room. "Um, so, you can sit wherever you want, I guess," Sabrina said to Sylvester as she gestured around the living room.

"Nah, I'm all right. I'll stand. Thank you, though, Miss Banner." He smiled.

Sabrina shrugged. "If you say so." Paris was already sitting on the loveseat couch, and Sabrina sat down beside her. She awkwardly twiddled her thumbs.

"I know this seems so sudden, and I apologize for intruding at such an early hour, but bad things are happening in my world. We need a hero—a savior—before it all goes to hell," Sylvester explained.

Sabrina abruptly stood up. "A hero? A savior? Excuse me, but who do you think you are? You do you think I am? I'm no one special. I'm not a hero or a savior. You must have the wrong person."

"You are so much more than what you give yourself credit for, Sabrina Banner. Maybe if we're lucky, you'll survive. You deserve to." Sylvester mumbles the last part quietly and he frowned before he shook his head again. "I've said too much. It's not the right time. Forgive me for confusing and worrying you. I'll be quiet now. No more secrets getting spilled." Sylvester firmed up his expression.

Sabrina opened her mouth to ask something, but Aunt Jeanette walked back into the room carrying an old wooden box with golden designs on it.

Aunt Jeanette blew on the box, and dust flew off of it, causing Paris to sneeze. "Sorry, Paris," Aunt Jeanette apologized.

Paris shrugged. "It's—ahchoo! It's fine." Paris sniffs.

Aunt Jeanette placed the box in Sabrina's hands. It was the size of an average shoebox. "This … This was your mother's. When she brought you to me that stormy night, so many years ago, she placed you in my arms. You were so little and you were swaddled up in an old brown blanket." Aunt Jeanette took a shaky breath and squeezed her eyes shut.

"Your mother—Aurora Banner—handed me this box and told me not to give it to you until it was time. She made me promise that I wouldn't. I knew who and what your father was, and yet I still questioned her logic. But I didn't argue. She told me that she loved me, and that she was sorry. My sister placed a kiss on your head and whispered, *'Forgive me, Sabrina. You're going to great things one day.'* A split second later there was a sharp, loud, high pitched howl."

A tear fell down Aunt Jeanette's cheek.

"Aurora paled. I had urged her to tell me what was going on, asking if she needed me to help her or if she was in trouble. Aurora told me not to worry, adding that it would be a while until we would see each other again. Then before I could say anything, she took off running into the pouring rain, before I could stop her and had disappeared into the darkness of the night. I stood there, holding you close to me and called her name. Seconds following that there was a shrilling scream ripped through the air. The howling stopped. The storm cleared up as if by magic. I called her name once more and got no response. I knew she was gone."

Sabrina let out a shaky breath that she hadn't known she had been holding. Sylvester hung his head, his eyes on glued to the ground as a tear slid down his cheek. Sabrina had never known the true story behind what had happened to her mom.

She had assumed that her mom simply hadn't wanted her, had died from an illness, or had had some sort of fatal accident. After Aunt Jeanette described how she had died, Sabrina suddenly felt guilty and numb.

In a voice barely above a whisper, Sabrina managed to ask, "And my dad?"

Sylvester raises his head and tilted it curiously. "What about your father?"

"What—what happened to him?" Sabrina pressed.

Aunt Jeanette and Sylvester shared a look and seemed to be having a private conversation that Sabrina couldn't translate. "I'm afraid that's a story for another time," Sylvester broke the silence. Sabrina frowned, not satisfied with the answer.

"Open the box, Sabrina," Aunt Jeanette murmurs gently, changing the subject.

Sabrina sighed slight annoyance as she pressed her lips together as she began to open up the box. It creaked ever so slightly with age, and more dust was inside the box. Sabrina had to blow the dust out, causing Paris to sneeze again.

Inside the box, Sabrina found a light purple journal with golden designs on its spine and cover. Its corner was slightly torn, and dirt stains were here and there.

Sabrina slowly picked up the book, and beneath it were old

black-and-white photos. She placed the book beside her and fished out the old photos.

One photo had a man kissing the cheek of a woman who had her hair up in a bun and a smile on her face. Sabrina put the picture aside to look at the next photo. This photo had the same man again, with his arms around the shoulders of a boy with messy raven black hair and a girl with neatly kept, ginger hair.

"That's me," Sylvester said as pointed to the man on the right side. "And that's your father. Then that's our old friend, Amaris Nightingale." Sylvester chuckled slightly, as if recalling a good memory.

Then his face darkened. "She's changed since then. Not the same Amaris that befriended Freddie and me. Oh, your father always hated it when we called him Freddie. Amaris started the nickname trend, and it caught on. Soon everyone started calling him it. Some did it to annoy him, and others did it because it was catchy. I did it because it made him scowl whenever I said it, and I knew he couldn't stay mad at me forever because we were best friends." Sylvester smiled faintly.

Sabrina nodded and looks at the other three remaining photos. She realized how they all wore the same outfit in each one, like a school uniform of sorts. However, Amaris's outfit was different from Sylvester's and Sabrina's dad's outfit.

Another photo was of her dad grinning like a child on Christmas morning as he wore that same purple uniform, except this time with a sky blue colored cape. Each of them wore a cape. It was the strangest thing Sabrina had ever seen. Grown men wearing capes? It didn't make sense, but Sabrina decided not to ask. The next photo, was of her father with a dog who looked like a golden retriever. Sylvester made it known to Sabrina that it was her mother's dog, named Cooper and her dad had just wanted a picture with the dog.

The last photo stopped Sabrina dead in her tracks. It was of her mom in a hospital bed, with Sabrina's dad sitting beside her, holding something small that was swaddled in his arms and smiling with pride. "Is—is that me?" Sabrina asked, surprised that her voice worked.

Sylvester nodded. "Yep, that's you. I'd never seen Fred more happy and proud than at that moment when he held you in his arms. I was the one who took the picture, come to think of it."

Sabrina turned her attention back to the box. The only things left were some old circular silver coins with a triangle engraved in the center of them. Sabrina didn't understand what they were for. She ignored them and gently placed the photos back inside, careful not to crease the pages.

"Oh, and that book was your mother's journal. She was always writing in it—documenting, was what she liked to call it." Sylvester recalled.

Sabrina smiled sadly as she fingered the little purple and gold journal. It was her first and only connection to her mother.

"Those were the good old days," Sylvester murmured pensively. Then he cleared his throat and clasped his hands together, rubbing them back and forth. "Well, I know that this is all very sudden and probably overwhelming, but it's almost four in the morning, and I've gotta get you to the Academy."

Sabrina furrowed her eyebrows together in puzzlement. "The Academy?"

"Yes, the Academy. It's in the Sorcerer Realm." Sylvester beamed.

"The Sorcerer Realm?" Sabrina repeated, closing the box and standing up.

Aunt Jeanette attempted to reason with Sylvester. "Sylvester, maybe we can wait until tomorrow. This is an awfully lot for one to take in."

"Jeanette, we can't wait. Sabrina needs to get to the Academy before noon."

Aunt Jeanette looked like she wanted to protest, but she let out a sigh of defeat. "All right, fine. Sabrina, please go pack a bag of clothes and items that you'll need, as if you were going on a vacation for a while."

Sabrina kept her eyebrows furrowed.

"A while? How long is, a while?" Paris replied for her, as if reading Sabrina's thoughts. Sabrina nodded in agreement.

Sylvester stroked his stubble chin and licked his lips in thought. "There really is no way to say. Just pack a few spare changes of clothes, a hairbrush, and things like that. No electronics allowed, because they won't work where we're going."

"Aunt Jeanette, you trust him? He could be lying. This guy could be some escapee from an asylum!" Sabrina exclaimed, waving her hands frantically.

Aunt Jeanette shook her head and smiled sadly. "He's not an escapee from an asylum, Sabrina. I'd know this man from anywhere. I've met him before. Besides, do you think I'd let a total stranger take you to some weird place even though he supposedly knows your father? No, absolutely not! I have common sense, Sabrina. Don't ever question that. Now, head up to your room and pack a bag of what Sylvester told you to pack, please."

Deciding that arguing with her would be useless, Sabrina sighed and made her way up the stairs to her bedroom.

II. "Fern Archer"

Sabrina entered her bedroom, still feeling overwhelmed by all that had happened.

She glanced at her alarm clock, and a groan escaped her lips as her eyes read the time: 5:32 a.m.

This is going to be a long day.

She'd be surprised if she didn't crash halfway through it. Sabrina quickly snatched her school backpack and dumped out all of her books.

Sabrina stuffed some outfits into the bag along with some hair bands, shoes, money, and the little blue box. Then she secretly slipped her phone into her pocket. Sabrina was well aware that Sylvester had said not to bring it, but it made her feel safer. If Sylvester did turn out to be some crazy man who had brainwashed her aunt into believing his lies, then at least she'd have a way of escape.

Sabrina quickly changed into a warm pair of clothes before she slung her backpack over her shoulders. She still didn't understand anything that was going on, but she knew that it involved her parents. With that in play, Sabrina was determined to learn more about them no matter the cost.

Sabrina put on a pair of sneakers and headed back out into the living room, deciding to ignore her messy bed-head hair for once. She was too tired to deal with it. Sylvester smiled when he saw Sabrina, and Sabrina took notice that he was suddenly wearing a dark forest green cape similar to the one that her dad had been wearing in the old photos.

Sylvester had his hands stuffed into the pockets of his brown trench coat and smiled weakly as their eyes locked. Sabrina didn't return the smile. She still didn't trust the guy, but who could blame her? He was a total stranger planning to take her to some realm, or whatever he called it. It was too crazy to make any sense of it at the moment. Maybe it was because it was so early, and her brain wasn't functioning properly yet. But whatever the case may be, Sabrina still wasn't grasping the concept of everything.

"I have so much to show you, Sabrina! Think of this little journey as a field trip, of sorts," Sylvester rambled, not helping Sabrina's uneasiness.

"Sylvester, you have places to be. You can explain more when you get there. Now, hurry along!" Aunt Jeanette chided as she shooed Sylvester with her hands.

"Yes, yes. I know we have to get going, blah, blah, blah," he mocked.

Aunt Jeanette glared at him. "I hate you so much." This was a whole new side to her that neither Paris nor Sabrina had ever seen.

"Mom, what's going on? I'm still confused," Paris remarked, and Sabrina nodded her head in agreement.

Aunt Jeanette sighed wearily. "I'll explain everything in the morning, Paris."

"But, it *is* morning," Paris argued.

Aunt Jeanette groaned and rubbed her temples. "Paris, please. Just go with it. And Sabrina, I wish you luck." Then she turned to Sylvester and spat, "You'd better make sure that she comes back in one piece." She embraced Sabrina tightly.

Sylvester raised his hands in defense. "She's the daughter of Freddie and Aurora. I can't make any promises, Jeanette."

Aunt Jeanette exhaled deeply and wiped her eyes. "Stay safe, Sabrina. Promise me, *please*," she murmured, placing a hand to Sabrina's cheek. "I'd never forgive myself if you didn't come back."

Sabrina's mind raced.

Didn't come back? What could be so dangerous where Sylvester is taking me? And if it's as dangerous as everyone is making it out to be, then why were we going there in the first place?

Sabrina wasn't one for making promises, and Aunt Jeanette knew that. But she looked so desperate, so pleading, that Sabrina knew she couldn't say no. "I—I promise," she weakly managed. She hoped that she wasn't lying. Sabrina didn't want to die. Like any normal person, she feared death and liked being alive.

"Good." Aunt Jeanette smiles and kissed Sabrina on the head before hugging her once more. "Keep me updated on everything that happens, all right, Sylvester?"

"Yes, ma'am!" Sylvester exclaimed, saluting to Sabrina's aunt like a soldier taking orders from his general.

"So where are we going?" Sabrina asked curiously.

Sylvester opened his mouth to reply when Paris tackled Sabrina from behind in a bone-crushing hug. "Don't I get a goodbye, Sea? You're like my sister. Don't die on me, all right? I don't know what the heck is going on around here, but I don't want you to wind up dead. Clear?"

"Crystal," Sabrina confirmed, and she gave Paris a clumsy captain's salute.

Paris laughed. "I'm holding you to that promise."

"I wouldn't expect anything else," Sabrina replied with a smile.

Sylvester interrupted. "Well, we should get going, Sabrina. It's heading to be six o'clock. We've got to get you to the Academy to sign in and all that jazz."

Sabrina nodded. "I'm still confused on what's going on, but I'm choosing to trust you."

"Excellent! Now come on. Let's head outside," Sylvester said as he made his way to the door.

"Take care, Sabrina!" Aunt Jeanette called out.

"Yeah! And don't die, Sea!" Paris added.

Sabrina forced a confident smile to her face as she waved goodbye to her family and followed Sylvester outside.

"So, where's your car?" Sabrina asked as she adjusted her shoulder straps on her backpack.

"My *car?* What a funny idea! Where we're going, we won't need a *car,*" Sylvester replied with an amused laugh.

Sabrina frowned. "*Won't need a car?* Then how else will we get there?"

Sylvester smirked, and a gleam of excitement flickered in his dusty blue eyes. "Like this. Take a hold of my hand, please, Sabrina." He held out his hand.

Sabrina reaches out and cautiously grabbed Sylvester's hand. With her free hand, Sabrina fingered her phone in her coat pocket. With her hand holding on to his, Sylvester rolled up the sleeve of his other hand to reveal a steam punk-styled wristwatch. He smiled. "And now the magic happens. Be sure to close your eyes—wouldn't want you burning up to a crisp. What you're about to experience may make you feel like you're going to die. It will be cold and will feel as though your body is ripping itself apart. But whatever you do, don't open your eyes. Now for the magic!"

Sabrina felt horror and confusion. "What mag—ah!"

A scream was torn from Sabrina's lips as coldness swept over her, and her body suddenly felt heavy, like she was being anchored to the ground.

She squeezed her eyes shut and felt nausea wash over her. Her heart started to race as cold wind brushed past her ears, causing her hair to fly all over the place. Sabrina had her mouth open to scream, but no sound came out.

Then the wind started to die down and the coldness began to melt. Sabrina felt sick to her stomach and extremely lightheaded. That was by far one of the worst things that she had ever experienced in her life. It was worse than a rollercoaster, and for Sabrina, that was saying something! Sabrina felt like her knees were going to collapse beneath her, as if she was too weak to support her own body weight.

"And we're here!" Sylvester exclaimed brightly while Sabrina groaned and clutched her stomach. "That was great, wasn't it, Sabrina?" He seemed much too cheerful.

"Oh, yeah. Just let me go back to grab my stomach," Sabrina grumbled. "Also, is everything else blurry and spinning for you?"

"Oh, no!" Sylvester panicked. Before Sabrina could make any response, she felt herself collapse, and her world went tumbling into a pit of everlasting darkness.

As it did before, Sabrina's body felt extremely cold. Sabrina felt herself slowly regaining consciousness, but she was so tired that she wanted to fall back asleep. She wasn't ready to wake up yet. Too many questions swarmed in her head. There was too much denial in her thoughts that made her wonder whether she was finally losing it.

Maybe she had hit her head really hard, and this was just a weird dream that came as a side effect. Sabrina could imagine the morning headlines: "Teenage Girl Hallucinates and Almost Dies from Running into a Tree."

Sabrina let out a groan of exhaustion and managed to groggily open her eyes.

"Ah, and Sleeping Beauty awakes!" a voice beside her joyfully exclaimed. It didn't take too long for her brain to match the voice to a person, allowing her to recognize that it was Sylvester.

"Wha—what happened?" she mumbled tiredly as she rubbed her eyes and slowly pushed herself up to a sitting position.

Sabrina realized that she was sitting on a cot with thin brown blankets on top of her and a small pillow underneath her head. Sabrina looked at her surroundings, and found Sylvester next to her, sitting in a fold-up chair beside the cot.

"You passed out. Don't worry, though. Realm traveling isn't for everyone at first. I'm surprised you didn't throw up! You're face was so green, and you looked horrible!" he recalled bluntly.

"Wow, thanks. I really wanted to remember that," Sabrina grumbled in annoyance.

Sylvester gave her a small smile and sheepishly rubbed the back of his neck. "Sorry. It's just ... you gave me quite a shock! You've been out for most of the day. But it's all right. I've got you checked in with a roommate, so all is taken care of." He spoke as if it to assure her, but Sabrina shook her head.

This is crazy.

Absolutely insane.

"Checked me in? Look, Sylvester. I still don't understand what's going on. You've explained nothing! One second we're in Denver, North Carolina, and the next we've been teleported to—where'd you say? Wait. Right now, where I am doesn't matter. What matters is that we've been teleported to a weird place! And teleporting? How on Earth is that even possible?"

Sylvester laughed. "You have much to learn, Sabrina. More than others. You were born of two worlds, one of magic and one of not. You're a sorceress, Sabrina Banner. The daughter of a legend! The prophecy child! You're practically famous to those who believe you exist!"

"*Famous?*" Sabrina screeched in shock. "*A sorceress?* No, no, no. This isn't possible! I'm not like Harry Potter, or anyone else with powers! Magic doesn't exist! I've finally cracked! I've gone completely mad!" She put her head in her hands and groaned.

"Harry who?" Sylvester asked with furrowed eyebrows.

"Harry Potter. A fictional character, meaning fake. Not real. Made up," she muttered.

"Well, I can assure you that this is real, Miss Banner. You're not going mad. We're in a realm, known as the Sorcerer Realm. There are plenty of other realms, such as the Spirit Realm and the Mortal Realm, which is the realm that you're from."

"What's the Sorcerer Realm?" Sabrina asked, having trouble wrapping her head around it. She propped herself into a more comfortable position, ignoring her faint headache.

"It's quite simple to understand, actually. I mean exactly what I said. We are no longer in the Mortal Realm, but we're in the Sorcerer Realm, and to pinpoint our location exactly, we are in the Academy's infirmary," Sylvester elaborated.

Sabrina groaned again. "Did I hit my head or something? How is this even possible to be in another realm? By a different realm, do you mean a different, dimension?" Sabrina asked, cocking her head in confusion.

Sylvester scoffed and crossed his arms. "No, I don't mean like a *dimension*." He attempted to mimic her voice. "No one seems to understand the difference between the two. There's a clear difference!" He huffed in annoyance.

Sabrina exhaled deeply and leaned back onto the pillows of the cot. "Then please, oh wise one, enlighten me." Sarcasm dripped from her voice.

"Firstly, a Realm is a place that is often parallel to something. For example the Sorcerer Realm is a parallel to the Mortal Realm and one can only reach it by what we Sorcerers call, Realm Traveling. So creative, believe me I know. But I wasn't the one who named it, thankfully. But anyways, two Realms work with each other and depend on each other for survival. If one goes, so does the other. A dimension is the exact opposite. A dimension is a place that a completely different from a Realm. Dimensions are like alternate realities that can be accessed usually through dreams. Like an optical allusion in some cases."

Sabrina raised an eyebrow. "Okay, so I'm going to pretend that I understood what you just said."

Sylvester sighed loudly and shook his head. He said in a defeated tone, "Why does no one understand this? It's such an easy concept to grasp ..."

Sabrina gave him a pat on the shoulder in fake sympathy, "Yeah, you just keep telling yourself that."

Sylvester rolled his eyes. "Anyway, do you think you can get out of bed? You have to change into the Academy uniform. If we hurry, you can catch dinner." He glanced down at his watch.

"What Academy?" Sabrina asked.

"So many questions! Why can't you just go with it? Curse the Mortal Realm. Curse it!" he grumbled. "The Academy is where you'll learn to master the magic of sorcery: hexes, jinxes, curses, transformations, allusions, morphing reality, and time travel. You'll even get your own cloak."

My own cloak? What? That doesn't make any sense! Why would I want a cloak? To play dress-up?

Sabrina decided to keep her questions to herself.

"Here." Sylvester picked up a pile of folded clothes that sat beside him and placed them in her arms. "Go get changed, and I'll explain more on the way to dinner." Just as he said *dinner*, Sabrina felt her stomach grumble in agreement.

Sabrina managed to get herself out of bed, despite how dizzy and overwhelmed she felt. So much was happening so quickly that it was almost impossible for her to grasp the situation at hand.

Almost.

The logical part of her was in denial and suggested that she had gotten a bad cold, which caused her to black out and have this weird dream. The fantasy part of her wanted to hold on to everything that happened, not wanting to let it go.

This was her chance to discover something that no one else had discovered before. This could be the adventure she had been waiting for.

But then a guilty thought came to mind. Sabrina had completely forgotten about her best friends, Demi and Jason. She should've made sure that Paris had a good excuse to tell them for her sudden disappearance.

They had made plans to hang out just about every day of their two-week spring break. But now that she was here (wherever *here* was), they couldn't do any of that.

All of that planning put to waste.

Sabrina wouldn't be surprised if they ignored her for a while, after she got back. *If* she got back.

No, not if.

When.

Sabrina mentally scolded herself for thinking so negatively. She was such a pessimist, as Paris liked to say, but she couldn't help it. Did she try to look on the bright side of things? Absolutely. But it was just … hard.

Sabrina was suddenly torn from her thoughts when she smacked foreheads with someone, causing her vision to momentarily blur.

She stumbled backwards.

Whoever she smacked heads with was clearly a male when he made a small groan on the quick impact. "Oh, my gosh, I'm so sorry. I was lost in thought and not paying attention to where I was going, and—" Sabrina began, but she was quickly cut off.

"Hey, it's fine. Accidents happen," the boy said.

Sabrina took the moment to actually look at the boy and his appearance. She noticed that he was kind of scrawny looking, with neatly brushed auburn hair and freckles across his nose and glasses with bright blue eyes.

"What are you staring at? Have I got something on my face?" he asked.

Sabrina felt heat rise to her cheeks. She hadn't realized that she had been staring. "Oh, no, I just … it's nothing. You're fine," Sabrina stammered, and she mentally cursed herself for sounding like such an idiot.

The boy gave her a lopsided, toothy smile, which Sabrina found slightly adorable.

What the heck was going on with her feelings?

"I'm Sage, by the way. Sage Jackson." He beamed. "I don't think I've seen you around here before—which is weird, because you look old enough to be in the Academy."

"I—I'm not from around here," Sabrina struggled to say.

"A newbie? That's weird. We never get newbies. Like … *ever*, unless of course you're a five year old, which clearly you are not. So where are you from?"

"To be frank, I have no idea what you refer to my home as around here. But according to my companion, I'm from the Mortal Realm." Sabrina replied, putting air quotes around the last words.

"You ...? The Prophecy ..." Sage said breathlessly with wide eyes.

Sabrina raised an eyebrow and hugged her uniform closer to her chest. "What prophecy?"

Sage sucked in a breath and closed his eyes. *"Born of mortal blood with magic in her veins, the daughter of a legend will soon begin her reign. She will journey far to seek what has been lost, but she will not return without a high cost. Betrayed by one she called friend, she will battle to the death, until the end."*

Sabrina blinked in shock and confusion, and he eyes fluttered back open, looking just as startled as before. *"You're* Sabrina Banner. I can't believe it! Man, Asher will be so jealous that I met you before he did!" He grinned like a kid on Christmas morning. His eyes were wide and full of excitement.

"Um." He stopped rambling and looked at Sabrina with a faint blush on his cheeks. It was kind of cute, in Sabrina's opinion. He sheepishly rubbed the back of his neck. "Sorry. I just ... wow. It's an honor to meet you, really. I can't believe that you're actually real."

Sabrina gave him a weak smile. "Well um, here I am. One hundred percent real. I think. And um, I don't understand what the big fuss is about me." she admitted.

"Well, I've never been to the Mortal Realm before, but I've read all about it. You're the first in centuries to be born of both a sorcerer and a mortal. It's forbidden, technically speaking."

"Great. I shouldn't exist. Hooray," Sabrina grumbled with fake enthusiasm.

"Oh, no, I didn't mean it like that! It's actually good that you're here, Sabrina. That means that the prophecy's going to come true soon, and we can't pull through the war without the Prophecy Child." Sage was clearly attempting to assure her, and Sabrina decided to try to not make him feel worse.

"It's fine, really. Can you show me where the bathroom is, please? I've got to get changed. I guess my companion wants me to try to catch dinner at the Academy."

Sage nodded sheepishly. "Yeah, sure. Follow me."

He led her past multiple cots that were lined up against the neutral-colored wall. Everything here seemed so depressing. After turning a corner, Sage eventually stopped in front of a door. "Here's the bathroom. Do you think you'll need help finding your way back?"

Sabrina shook her head. "No, I'll manage. Thanks."

Sage gave her small smile that seemed meant to be a way of apologizing before turning around and disappearing behind the corner.

Sabrina exhaled deeply and went into the bathroom, changing into the uniform. It consisted of a long-sleeved, buttoned-up, collared royal purple shirt with knee-high royal purple socks and black dress shoes.

On the shirt, there was a crest that was in the shape of a medieval shield with a crescent moon on one side and a single star on the other. The crest was outlined in gold, and there were various other parts of the uniform that had gold accents.

As much as Sabrina hated skirts, she told herself to at least try to be positive and be thankful that the uniform wasn't pink. She left the bathroom and managed to make her way back to the cot she had been recovering on.

She found Sylvester impatiently tapping his foot with his arms crossed over his chest in annoyance. "There you are! Took ya long enough! Come on, kid! Dinner starts in twenty minutes, and you still have to get settled in with your new roommate!"

Sabrina quickly slid her backpack straps onto her shoulders, and Sylvester grabbed her wrist and pulled her out of the infirmary.

Sabrina caught Sage staring at her from across the room, and the prophecy that Sabrina had just heard came to mind.

She decided that Sylvester was jumpy and impatient enough, and so she didn't need to get on his bad side. She kept it to herself. Eventually, though, she wanted answers. And one way or another, Sabrina would get answers.

The infirmary led to a long hallway with walls made of cobblestone and the floor made of cold cement. "Where are we?" Sabrina asked in awe as torches were mounted to the wall and dimly lit the passageway.

"In the Academy, duh. Where else? Man, who knew that I was going to have to explain so much to you? Good grief. If I had known, I would've brought along the school handbook! But no matter. I think we're managing pretty well," Sylvester rambled as he pulled out some papers from his trench coat pocket. He unfolded the papers as they walked down the hallway.

Then he mumbled to himself, trying to figure out which paper was for what.

"Man, Amaris. Why must you make everything so complicated? The school was perfectly fine the way it was. You've made so many changes since I left, and now none of this makes any sense!"

Sabrina was left more confused than ever. She wanted to ask questions, but she decided that keeping her mouth shut and staying on Sylvester's good side would probably be her best bet.

I will get answers later, she kept reminding herself.

Sylvester continued to mumble as he took turns glancing between the papers in his rough hands and the doors that they passed. The doors were beautiful, and it made her wonder what they led to. Golden numbers marked each door in numerical order. Even numbers were on the right, and odd numbers were on the left.

Eventually, Sylvester halted to a sharp stop, and Sabrina nearly bumped into him. She managed to catch herself before she crashed into Sylvester or fell backward and landed on her butt. "Ah, here we are. Room thirteen!" he remarked as he spun around to face her with a smile.

Sabrina frowned and furrowed her eyebrows. "Room thirteen? Isn't that bad luck or something?"

Sylvester laughed. "Only to those who believe in superstitions." He waved his hand in dismissal. "Well, we should probably knock. Wouldn't want to startle your new roommate and get off on the wrong foot." He grinned as he knocked on the door.

A minute or so later, the door swung open, revealing a girl with ginger hair. The color slightly reminded Sabrina of Demi's hair, but it wasn't nearly as curly. The girl had her hair pulled back into a high pony and she wore the same uniform as Sabrina.

"Oh, my gosh! You must be my new roommate! Amaris told me to expect a new roommate soon. I'm so excited!" The girl suddenly grabbed Sabrina's arm and pulled her into the room, causing Sylvester to be shoved aside.

Man, what is it with people pulling me around by my arm?

Sabrina thought in annoyance.

First Paris at three o'clock in the morning, then Sylvester, and now this girl, who apparently is my new roommate.

"Who's the guy in the trench coat?" Sabrina's new roommate whispered to her, eyeing Sylvester suspiciously.

"Oh, um, that's Sylvester. My … escort, I suppose," Sabrina awkwardly replied.

The girl raised an eyebrow in suspicion as if not believing what Sabrina had said. Then she grinned again and let go of Sabrina's arm.

The girl moved to where Sylvester was, yanked him into the room as well, and closed the door shut behind him. Sylvester stood off to the side, letting the two girls talk. He seemed lost in thought.

"Well, welcome to your new room, new bestie!" Then she briefly looked as if she was mentally scolding herself. "Please call me Archer. Fern Archer." She beamed. "And you are …?"

"Oh! Um, Sabrina Banner," Sabrina replied with a nod.

Fern's eyes widened.

Sabrina thought, *Oh, no.*

Another person who's going to fawn over me and go on about how famous I supposedly am. Or how I'm not supposed to exist. Or that I'm going to be some big hero or something.

Great.

Just.

Great. She sighed in exasperation.

"Oh, my god! You're *the* Sabrina Banner? As in the daughter Frederick and Aurora Banner? That's amazing! I can't believe that I get to be your roommate! *This is incredible!*" Fern stopped fangirling, and heat rose to her cheeks. "Oh, my goodness, I'm so sorry, Sabrina. I didn't—I don't mean to overwhelm you or anything. It's an honor to meet you and an even bigger honor to be your roommate. I hope that we can be friends."

Sabrina smiles weakly. "As do I," she partly lied. "And it's fine, really. You're not the first person who's done that. I would love to be your friend. I'll need some help finding my way around this new world, anyway."

Fern gave a small smile of gratitude. "You're so humble and kind. You're going to do great things, Sabrina Banner. I can just feel it!" She gave a stiff nod.

"Um, I hate to break up this little bonding moment, but dinner starts in ten minutes, and I have no idea as to where the dining hall is. It's been years since I've been here!" Sylvester exclaimed.

Fern laughed. "Relax! I know a shortcut to the dining hall. By the way, that's your bed over there. You can buy bed sheets of your choice, as well as room decor at the Academy store. I can show you tomorrow during our hour of downtime after lunch."

Sabrina nodded before she went over to the left side of the room to place her bag on her bed. She stole a glance at Fern's side of the room and noticed how bright and colorful it was. Stuffed animals and many pillows covered her bed, and flower stickers decorated the dusty blue walls.

Fern said, "Now, just follow me, and I'll lead the both of you to the dining hall. Come on! We've got seven minutes to get there, or we'll be marked late."

III. "Dragon Eyes and Unicorn Hair"

Sabrina had never felt so many emotions at once.

So many thoughts went through her head as Fern led her and Sylvester to the dining room.

"And here we are!" Fern said happily. After walking down long, winding hallways that looked the same, the trio finally reached another pair of giant doors that automatically opened as they approached. It reminded Sabrina of automatic doors at a superstore. The three walked inside, and Sabrina's eyes widened.

Everything was so fancy.

Multiple long, wooden tables were scattered across the room in rows, with decorative cream-colored tablecloths. Silver plates with delicate glass cups lined the tables, along with silverware that was wrapped neatly up in silk napkins. A huge chandelier dangled overhead in the center of the hexagon-shaped dining room, and a platform was in the center of the room and held the longest table.

The chairs were like thrones and gave Sabrina an odd déjà vu feeling.

"This place is beautiful," she breathed, awestruck.

Fern giggled and replied, "Of course it is! The headmistress, Mrs. Nightingale, loves this kind of style. Almost everything in the Academy has a touch of elegance and fanciness to it."

"*Mrs.* Nightingale?" Sylvester repeated in shock.

"Mmm-hmm," Fern confirmed. "She married a man named Anthony

Nightingale, who was a very skilled sorcerer. Unfortunately, he died—killed by Caspian in the big battle twenty years ago, leaving the headmistress and her son on their own." Fern's nose scrunched up in disgust. "Her son is a jerk. He's such a snobby, stuck-up, no-good brat who thinks he gets everything he wants. He makes everyone feel like trash, and Headmistress treats him like a prince, completely oblivious to his bratty attitude."

"What's his name?" Sabrina asked, so that she knew to avoid him when she saw him. "Nicholas Nightingale. Call him Nick, and he'll ruin your life. No joke. Don't think I'm just trying to trick you or anything" Fern states firmly, and Sabrina nodded.

"Sylvester Coulson?" a surprised female voice asked from behind the trio. Fern swallowed nervously as they turned to greet the visitor.

"Amaris?" Sylvester squeaked.

A very slim lady with an hour-glass like body shape was dressed in a royal purple suit that matched the uniform colors. She had dark brown hair that was pulled back into an elegant bun with chocolate brown eyes and pale skin.

She walked slowly toward the group, her heels tapping against the hard floor. The woman had a silver cape that was majestically blowing behind her. "What are you doing back here? You know that you're forbidden from coming here," she hissed.

"I'm just dropping off a new student. I promised Freddie that I would, and I wasn't going to bail on him. Not my best friend. Not again," Sylvester replied sternly, crossing his arms over his chest. "Now, go ahead. Kick me out if you want, Amaris. But that just goes to show the cold-hearted person that you've turned out to be. Freddie would be disappointed."

Amaris glared at Sylvester, but she quickly composed herself. Sabrina sensed an old rivalry between the two, but she chose not to comment on it.

"I've chosen my path, and he chose his, Coulson. He chose to break the rules. It's not my fault that he vanished," Amaris spat back, with her arms crossed and her nose up in the air.

"I never said it was. No need to jump to conclusions, Amaris. Anyway, Sabrina, this is—" Sylvester began, but Amaris cut him off.

"You should be dead," Amaris suddenly interjected.

Sabrina felt her blood run cold and her body becomes numb. "E-excuse me?" she stammered.

"That's enough, Amaris!" Sylvester jumped in, protectively standing in front of Sabrina. "Now is not the right time or place to discuss that." He gestured to the other people in the room who were staring at them with interest.

"Fine," Amaris huffed, and Sylvester crossed his arms in annoyance. Amaris's eyes locked on Sabrina's before she said, *"This* is Fred's daughter? She looks a lot more like Aurora. She has Fred's eyes, though." She directly addressed Sabrina. "Please excuse me, for my, um, actions earlier, but it's a pleasure to meet you, Miss Banner. I'm sure you're very overwhelmed by all that's happened within such a short period of time, but just go with the flow, and I'm sure Miss Archer can help you adjust into your new lifestyle."

Fern nodded her head in agreement.

"Now, why don't you and Miss Archer go to a table to prepare to eat? Dinner will begin shortly. I have some business that I need to take care of." Amaris glared at Sylvester, and it made Sabrina feel bad for the guy. She wanted to stay here and learn more about their past with her father.

However, Fern once again grabbed her arm and led her away. "Come on, Sabrina. You can sit next to my friend and me."

"Um, yeah, okay," Sabrina replied, still feeling overwhelmed.

Fern and Sabrina wove their way around tables, and Sabrina got a few glances of curiosity from others whom they passed.

Sabrina's eyes scanned the room as she saw people from age five to eighteen sitting at the tables, chatting and deep in conversation. Sabrina felt people's eyes on the back of her neck as she continued to let Fern guide her.

She tried to ignore the anxiety creeping up in her stomach, and she focused more on everything else around her. Sabrina also noticed that almost everyone wore a cape, or cloak as Sylvester put it.

Sabrina made a mental note to herself to stop calling it a cape and start calling it a cloak. If she ended up getting one, she didn't want to look like an idiot and misidentify it all the time.

Eventually, Sabrina and Fern reached a table where a girl with long straight brown hair sat, her back facing them.

The girl wore a lavender cloak with a high collar. Fern tapped the girl gently on her shoulder shoulder, and the girl turned and smiled.

"Hi, Fern." Her voice was gentle and soft, as if she didn't want to disturb anyone.

"Hey, Aureum," Fern replied. "Sabrina, meet my friend, Aureum Cor. Aureum, meet Sabrina Banner, my new roommate and friend."

Aureum? What an odd name. It's really different, yet pretty at the same time, Sabrina thought. Sabrina gave Aureum a small wave. Aureum smiled warmly and gave Sabrina a welcoming nod of her head.

"Mind if Sabrina sits between us?" Fern asked.

"No, not at all. Go right ahead," Aureum replied quietly.

"All right, Sabrina. You can sit here, and I'll sit on the other side of you," Fern said, pulling Sabrina from her thoughts. Fern sat down a seat away from Aureum.

"Thanks," Sabrina said with a grateful smile as she took a seat between Aureum and Fern. She glanced over her shoulder to see Sylvester storming out of the room with his hands stuffed in his pockets and a grumpy expression on his face.

Amaris looked a little shaken, but she did well of quickly covering it.

Sabrina watched Amaris make her way up to a platform that was separated from the other tables, where other adults sat.

She stood at the end of the long table and lifted her cup. Amaris gently tapped her spoon against the glass, and the room went silent in record time.

"Good evening, students. I hope you all had a good day with your classes and training. As usual, before we eat, I'd like to welcome the new members to the Academy. As I say every night, you will treat every member old and new, with respect, and I want no messing around. You are here to learn. You are here to keep the Realms in balance and safe. Am I understood?"

Nods and murmurs of agreement rippled across the room.

"Good. I will now announce our new members in alphabetical order. When I say your name, please rise so that you can be seen."

Sabrina felt heat rise to her cheeks, and her stomach become a little queasy. She hated being the center of attention. Standing up in front of all these strangers would surely now be the death of her. Sabrina felt the palms of her hands get sweaty, and her heart hammered so hardly against her chest.

She hated people staring at her.

Maybe it was because of her anxiety, but she couldn't help it.

"Timothy Andrews," Amaris began.

A young boy of around five or six with shaggy black hair stood.

"Melissa Anthony."

Sabrina watched a girl with short brown hair rise.

She was around the same age as Timothy and looked just as nervous as she felt.

"And Sabrina Banner."

Sabrina shakily rose, feeling awkward because she was the oldest one who had stood up.

She trembled so badly that she felt like her knees would buckle. The moment she stood up, she heard whispers and murmurs across the room, making her feel even more anxious to sit back down.

"You may now all sit. And without further ado—" Amaris began, but she was cut off when all of a sudden, two girls rose, holding hands and not blinking. One girl had bright blue eyes with really curly blonde hair, and the other had long, straight black hair with bangs that cascaded over one of her gray eyes.

"Oh, no," Fern murmured quietly.

"Girls, please, sit down," Amaris practically pleaded.

They didn't listen. Sabrina raised an eyebrow quizzically.

"Hex, Jinx, sit down," Amaris demanded again.

They still stood.

Then their eyes glowed white, and they spoke in perfect unison.

"Born of mortal blood with magic in her veins, the daughter of a legend will soon begin her reign. She will journey far to seek what has been lost, but she will not return without a high cost. Betrayed by one she called friend, she will battle to the death, until the end."

The whole room was in dead silence.

Sabrina kept her gaze at the empty plate in front of her, trying to hide herself and wishing that she could melt into the floor and vanish. It was so quiet that one could hear a pin drop. Their eyes returned to normal, and they both looked confused.

"Did we just …?" The girl with curly blonde hair began as she glanced at the girl with straight black hair. "Give a prophecy?" the girl with the straight black hair finished.

Amaris said, "Yes, you both did. Now, everyone, don't worry. Yes, Hex and Jinx both just gave us a very ..." The headmistress awkwardly cleared her threat. "I know that you all are probably a little shaken. I know that it's been years since anyone's spoken of the prophecy, but you needn't worry. Everything will be fine."

That didn't stop the uneasy nervousness that everyone felt, and the students whispered among themselves.

"Banner?"

"Prophecy come true?"

"Prophecy child?"

"Not supposed to exist?"

"Daughter of Frederick and Aurora Banner!"

"Everyone, hush up! I will here no more of this matter. Yes, the daughter of Frederick and Aurora Banner is here. Yes, she is the only one of her kind to come to our realm. Yes, that does mean that it is only a matter of time before Caspian strikes. And yes, the prophecy will eventually come true. But no, we will not make a big fuss about it. Everything will go as it always does. No one will bombard Miss Banner with questions. She doesn't need any more stress than what she is already under. Got it?" Amaris demanded.

Small nods of agreement could be seen throughout the room, and a horrible knot of fear formed in the pit of Sabrina's stomach.

This is absolute madness.

This has to be a dream.

It just has to be!

Her hand traveled to the little pocket of her skirt uniform, where she'd put her phone when she'd changed outfits. She fingered the screen with a racing heart as she recalled that her phone was a reminder that this was real. This was actually happening. Still, despite the minor reassurance, Sabrina still questioned her sanity.

"No more discussion about this. You are free to eat," Amaris concluded with a curt nod. Quiet conversations began, and Sabrina could feel people's eyes burning into the back of her head. She exhaled deeply in an attempt to calm her unsettled nerves.

Sabrina turned her attention back to her plate and glass, causing her to gasp in shock when food magically appeared on Aureum's plate. Following that, food appeared on other people's plates.

"Wait! Whoa, how did you do that?" Sabrina exclaimed in bewilderment and awe. Aureum smiled faintly, and Fern laughed.

"It's easy, Sabrina," Aureum began in a quiet voice. "Just look at your plate, say what you want to eat, and then poof! It's there."

Sabrina gave Aureum a look that clearly said, '*You're nuts*'

Aureum simply smiled in reply. "Just try it," she urged.

Fern nodded her head in agreement. Sabrina let out a sigh of exasperation, realizing that she was fighting a battle she couldn't win—and that she was too hungry to argue. She looked at her plate and said, "Grilled cheese with French fries." The split second after she said it, the food that she had asked for appeared on my plate.

Sabrina's eyes widened. "Wow, that's incredible! But my only question is … does it taste as good as it looks?"

Fern laughed. "I guess that's for you to find out. I can't believe that they don't have this in the Mortal Realm. Man, how I wish I could see that realm sometime …" She sighed pensively.

"Well, why don't you?" Sabrina asked as she picked up her grilled cheese.

Fern sighed and tucked a stray piece of her ginger bangs behind her ear. "It's forbidden and dangerous. Mortals can't know about the magic barrier that we sorcerers use to keep magic out of their world. They can't know about all of the magic that we shield them from because their brains can't process it all. It would drive them mad!"

Sabrina knitted her eyebrows together in puzzlement. "Then why haven't I gone mad? I've been questioning my sanity ever since I arrived here in the infirmary!"

"I think Aureum should answer that question. She's better at explaining this kind of stuff then I am," Fern admitted.

Sabrina nodded and turned her attention to Aureum, who had noodles on her plate.

"It's complicated, Sabrina," Aureum began slowly, her voice still quiet and gentle.

Sabrina sighed and grumbled, "Everything suddenly seems so complicated."

Aureum gave Sabrina a look of sympathy before saying, "Since you were born from a sorcerer and a mortal, you were born with two souls."

"Two souls? Wait, what?" Sabrina cried, clearly flabbergasted.

"It means that one of your souls is the source of your sorcerer magic, which you have yet to learn and master. It was the soul that you got from your father. Then you have your mortal soul from your mother, which allows you to blend in more easily in the Mortal Realm than it would for us. If you get injured to the point of death, it'll be like you have two lives. Your sorcerer's soul will act like a shield and vanish, taking your powers with it."

Sabrina's head was pounding.

This was so confusing and messed up.

I have two souls? I have two chances to live? That's so weird. Yet it's cool at the same time. Sabrina let out a shaky sigh and nodded. "That's confusing, but I think I get the concept. How do you know that though?" "Ley's just say that the Prophecy interested me a lot when I was younger and I did a lot of research on it." Aureum responded and Sabrina nodded.

"Good now that we cleared that up. Let's eat before our food gets cold," Fern chided. Aureum and Sabrina obliged and dug into their meals.

Thankfully, dinner finished more quickly than Sabrina had expected. Fern and Sabrina bid Aureum a good night and made their way back to their dorm.

Someone called Sabrina's name and placed a hand on her shoulder. Sabrina quickly spun around on her heel to find the headmistress standing behind her. "Miss Archer, you can go ahead to your dorm. I want to speak with Miss Banner in private."

Fern glanced at Sabrina, and Sabrina gave her a small nod of her head, telling Fern that it was okay. Fern glanced at the headmistress before turning around and quickly making her way toward their dorm.

"Please follow me, Miss Banner," Amaris ordered.

Knowing that she was someone whom Sabrina would want as an ally, not as an enemy, Sabrina obliged and followed closely next to her. Students passed them in large groups, and Sabrina felt like a fish swimming upstream. But the moment that people saw Amaris Nightingale, they immediately made way for her.

Sabrina noticed how Amaris walked with elegance and poise. Her posture was practically perfect, and she kept her hands folded neatly together. It was like she was royalty, given how she carried herself.

"You're not in trouble, Miss Banner. I just wanted to talk to you. Aside from Mr. Coulson, I was a close friend of your father," Amaris began as they continued to walk down dimly lit passageway.

Sabrina couldn't hold it back anymore.

She was furious at Amaris for sending away Sylvester. Sylvester might have been her only hope in ever finding her dad, and it turned out he was not allowed in the Academy.

"Speaking of which, why did you send away Sylvester? He wasn't doing anything wrong, other than making sure I got here safely. He was explaining how things work around here, and without him, I have no idea as to what I'm supposed to be doing. He made my dad a promise, and if you care about my dad, then you'll let Sylvester back into the Academy. You're all supposed to be friends—I saw pictures of all you. None of this makes sense!" she blurted, shocking Amaris (and herself) with her sudden outburst.

Sabrina hadn't meant to say all of that, but it just happened.

"You don't know what Sylvester, Frederick, and I have been through, Sabrina Banner. I suggest you don't go sticking your nose where it doesn't belong. And for your information, Sylvester and your father were expelled from the Academy when we were younger, a year before we all were suppose to graduate. It was because Sylvester and your father snuck off to the Mortal Realm, which led to your father meeting your mother." Amaris took a shaky breath.

"A lot has happened, since then, Miss Banner. I miss your father deeply. I don't know what happened to him or know of his whereabouts. I advise you not to ask more about it. It's a subject that I do not wish to speak about. Sylvester might want to, but not me. Fredrick is gone, and that's that. Now you're here, and a prophecy has been released. It's my job to make you into who you're supposed to be to fulfill that prophecy. Do as I say, stay out of trouble, and make as many allies as you can, and all should be well. Do you understand?"

Sabrina gave her a silent nod.

"Good. Now, off to your dorm. Classes start at nine o'clock sharp and go to four. I can't have you falling asleep on your first day at the Academy.

You may not realize it yet, but you have just as many enemies as you do followers."

"But I don't even know anyone here! How could I have enemies and followers already? And what are we even fighting? Why do I have to be the hero? Why couldn't I have learned about this sooner?" Sabrina asked, running her hand through her short and wavy blonde hair in frustration.

"This is exactly why no one told you, sooner, Sabrina," Amaris said slowly, using Sabrina's first name for once. "We feared that if you found out sooner, you would have to grow up faster. It wouldn't be fair to expect you to know how to wield magic like a true sorcerer when you have both—"

"A Mortal's soul and a Sorcerer's soul." Sabrina interrupted, remembering what Aureum had told her.

Amaris's eyes widened in shock and she stopped walking to face Sabrina. "How did you …?"

"A new friend of mine explained it to me. I was questioning how I was still sane, and it was explained to me. I don't know whether I believe the whole thing just yet, to be frank," Sabrina admitted.

Amaris nodded slowly. "Well, that's all that we need to discuss for now. If you have any more questions, ask one of your friends or my son, Nicholas. You've probably heard of him by now, yes?"

Sabrina nodded.

"I suppose that I should lead you back to your dorm, seeing as how you'd probably be up all night trying to find it. Come along." Amaris began walking back in the direction that they had come from. Sabrina was tempted to retort that she wouldn't get lost, but she knew Amaris was right.

For Sabrina to remember something or some place that she'd been to, she had to do it over and over again before it stuck in her head.

Sabrina decided to keep her distance from Amaris and let the woman have the full lead. Meanwhile, Sabrina's brain wandered to the prophecy.

Just the thought of it made her want to curl up into a ball under her covers and hide from everything.

Born of mortal blood with magic in her veins, the daughter of a legend will soon begin her reign. She will journey far to seek what has been lost, but she will not return without a high cost. Betrayed by one she called friend, she will battle to the death, until the end. Sabrina let out a deep breath.

It didn't make any sense.

She pressed her lips tightly together in thought.

Amaris came to a stop, and Sabrina stopped as well before she smacked into her. "Well this is your dorm, room thirteen." Amaris paused and stared at the door for a moment. Her eyebrows furrowed, and her eyes glued to the number written on it.

"Oddly enough ..." she muttered under her breath, as if remembering something unpleasant. She began to leave.

Sabrina yelled, "Wait!"

Amaris turned around. "Yes?"

"The—the prophecy. It doesn't make any sense, except for maybe the first line. How am I supposed to save the world and fulfill this prophecy, if I can't even decipher it?"

Amaris was quiet for a moment. "I will help you, Sabrina. If I don't, not only your realm but also mine will perish and fall to evil. Even if I don't like your kind, I won't lose my people over my dislikes. If I discover anything, I will inform you at once. But you have to do your part. I know this is confusing and a lot to take in, but everyone here—"

"Expects me to be the hero. I know," Sabrina finished.

Amaris looked surprised for a second, but nods. "Right. As of now, though, if he were to try and waltz into the Academy, demanding whatever it is that he wants, we would all likely perish. You would be killed, and we can't have that. So promise me that you will try more than your best to learn our ways and master your magic," Amaris said in a dead-serious voice.

Sabrina really hated making promises, especially when there was not a one hundred percent guarantee that she could fulfill them.

But she'd been making a lot promises with possible what-if scenarios, and so one more couldn't hurt, could it?

Sabrina let out a shaky breath, still not completely grasping the whole situation but agreeing to it anyways. It was her first mistake.

"I promise."

Amaris seemed slightly reassured and more relaxed. "Good. Miss Archer, and any other friends that you manage to make, will help you find your way around the Academy tomorrow. I suggest you be on time for most if not all classes, because the teachers aren't always very forgiving. I will help you in my spare time when I can, but no one must know of it.

Do you understand? There will be consequences for both you and me if you choose to ignore my warning."

Sabrina bit her tongue to avoid letting out a sigh of exasperation and nodded her head.

"I'm glad that I make myself clear. Until tomorrow, Miss Banner."

Sabrina watched Amaris walk down the hallway past other dorms that held sleeping students of the Academy.

Sabrina ran a hand through her hair and mentally cursed herself for making so many promises. She needed to stop. She let out a breath, her shoulders slumping in exhaustion as she turned the doorknob and pushed open the door.

"Sabrina, you're back! Oh, thank goodness! I thought you were in deep trouble already—and you haven't even spent a full day here yet!" Fern rambled.

Sabrina walked into the room, groggily rubbing her eyes. "She just wanted to talk, Fern."

"About the prophecy?" Fern asked as she tilted her head. Her voice dropped to a whisper, as if people would overhear.

"Eh, sort of. We talked a little bit about that, but it was nothing that you need to worry about. Everything's fine, really. Hey, could you tell me where the bathroom is? I haven't had the time to go, and I really need to shower," Sabrina said, changing the subject.

"Oh, yeah. We have a bathroom in our room with a shower. Just go through that door, and you'll find the bathroom," Fern responded as she pointed to a door that was on the side of the room, away from their twin-sized beds.

"Thanks." Sabrina got a pair of pajamas out of the bag that she had brought from home.

"Whoa, Mortal Realm stuff ... *Awesome!*" Fern had wide eyes filled with awe. "You've got to tell me all about the Mortal Realm sometime, Sabrina. I have so many questions"

Sabrina beamed. "Sure thing. As long as in exchange, you can tell me about the Sorcerer Realm." She reached to open the bathroom door while hugging her pajamas to her chest.

Fern replied, "Sounds like a deal."

The girls exchanged smiles before Sabrina opened the bathroom door and walked inside.

The sun rose over the distant horizon. Sabrina didn't sleep well that night. She didn't know what time she had managed to fall asleep, but it hadn't been for long.

"—brina, Sabrina. Sabrina, wake up, or you're going to be late!" Fern's high-pitched voice chided as she whacked Sabrina on the back with one of her pillows.

"Let me sleep," Sabrina groaned, burying her face further into her pillow.

"No! I don't want to be late! Get up!" Fern retorted.

Sabrina felt her blanket be pulled away from her, causing her to bolt up into a sitting potion. "Hey! What was that for?"

"To get you out of bed. Now, get dressed and get ready for breakfast, because we leave in fifteen minutes," Fern answered.

Sabrina groaned in response and rolled out of bed. She landed painfully on her stomach, causing her to groan in pain again.

"Ow," Sabrina whined as she pushed herself up to her feet. "Fern, what am I supposed to wear? All I have are some clothes from my home and the one uniform from yesterday." She saw Fern making her bed on the other side of the room.

"At the end of your bed, there's a chest. Open it up and you'll find some more uniforms in there," Fern replied, her eyes not diverting from the blanket she was smoothing as she pointed toward the end of Sabrina's bed.

Sabrina trudged over to the chest at the end of her bed and grunted while pushing it open. It was kind of heavy, and this would easily become a pain opening and closing it every morning and evening when she needed clothes.

Sabrina went into the bathroom and quickly tossed on the purple and gold uniform, which resembled the one she wore yesterday. Sabrina begrudgingly put on the skirt, and instead of slipping on the black flats that came with it, she put on her sneakers from home instead. Then Sabrina's hand went to pick up her phone that she had placed on the edge of the sink.

When Sabrina's fingers wrapped around it, she furrowed her eyebrows and turned it on. The battery was a little below 100 percent, and there were no recent messages as there usually would be. Sabrina checked for service in the top corner; as she had expected, there was none.

"Sabrina, hurry up! Five minutes left!" Fern's voice rang out.

Sabrina quickly shut off her phone, put it into her pocket, and snatched her brush as she left the bathroom. Sabrina saw Fern standing there with an impatient expression on her face, waiting for her with books clutched to her chest.

"Let's go, Sabrina!" Fern yelled.

Sabrina quickly brushed her hair and made sure she had everything she need. "We'll probably get points off because your bed's a mess, but we don't have the time to stay and make it," Fern grumbled as she opened the door.

Sabrina frowned. "What points?"

Fern waved her hand in dismissal and replied, "It doesn't matter right now! What matters is that we're not late for breakfast, so let's go!" She grinned and rushed out door.

Sabrina exhaled deeply before tossing her hair brush onto her bed and running after Fern.

Sabrina soon found herself sitting between Fern and Aureum like the night before, and she had eggs with sausage.

The food reminded her of Aunt Jeanette's cooking, but perhaps she was just imagining it because she was homesick.

Amaris caught up with Sabrina during breakfast and gave her the schedule that she would use to get around to her new classes.

Sabrina learned that most who attended the Academy began at age five and leveled up based upon abilities, experience and completed missions or quests. Amaris explained that because Sabrina had started late, she have a couple classes with kids who were probably younger than her. Even though it kind of bugged Sabrina, she pretended that she was fine with it because she had no room to argue.

She didn't know anything about the Sorcerer's Realm.

She was a complete stranger.

After talking with Amaris, Sabrina talked with Aureum and Fern to figure out her schedule and get a feel as to where her classes were. Surprisingly, she only had four classes, unlike back home where she would've had eight.

Sabrina learned that she had three out of the four classes with Aureum and two with Fern. According to Amaris, she needed to work hard and catch up quick with everyone. Amaris said that sometime soon, they would talk, and Amaris would explain the prophecy and more about the Academy later.

Sabrina learned that the Academy was called just that.

No name followed it. It struck Sabrina as odd, but she didn't question it.

To make things even more confusing, there was no time for when each class began or ended. There were no classroom numbers or a map of the Academy. Fortunately, Sabrina could follow Aureum around for most of her classes, if Aureum didn't mind.

Sabrina sighed as she and Aureum walked side by side in the hallway, passing other students rushing around to get to class or playing pranks on each other with magic. All of them wore cloaks, but each cloak was a different color and maybe a slightly different style. No cloak was exactly the same. It reminded Sabrina of zebras with their strips. Sabrina sighed and said to Aureum, "I don't understand any of these classes."

"Don't worry. You'll catch on soon enough. Everyone does," Aureum said.

Sabrina nodded, not feeling completely assured but not wanting to hurt Aureum's feelings. Aureum was simply being nice. Sabrina hadn't noticed it before, but around Aureum's waist she wore a bronze belt, similarly styled to a tool belt—but instead of tools being in it, there were small, differently shaped glass vials filled with colorful liquids.

Sabrina assumed that they were potions because she was currently in a world where magic existed, but still she made a mental note to herself to ask about it later.

As they continued to make their way to their first lesson, Sabrina admired the interior design of the Academy.

It was all fancy and elegant, with a medieval touch to it. It faintly reminded Sabrina of Harry Potter and Hogwarts. The Academy was rather beautiful, Sabrina had to admit. It made her wonder what the exterior of it looked like as well as what the Sorcerer Realm itself looked like.

"So, our teacher for our first class—"

"Lesson," Aureum interrupted, correcting Sabrina.

Sabrina cleared her throat and nodded slowly. "Right, *lesson*. It's Alchemy with Madam Rhea?"

"Yes, that is correct," Aureum confirmed with a slight nod of her head.

"Thanks. I don't mean to be annoying or anything. I just … I need to get a feel of this place. It's very different from home," Sabrina replied as she rubbed the back of her neck.

Aureum smiled and laughed a little. "Don't worry about it, Sabrina. Any friend of Fern's is a friend of mine. Well, after you gain my trust, that is. I don't do well with meeting new people and making friends, but you seemed nice, so here we are."

Sabrina felt a smile form on her lips as well. "That's relatable. Back home, I only have two real friends and my cousin to hang out with. I'm not considered cool or popular in the Mortal Realm." Sabrina laughed, although Aureum gave her a confused look.

"But … but you're Sabrina Banner! How could you not be popular in the Mortal Realm? So many sorcerers here would kill to meet you, others envy you, and some fear you, a good lot think you to be just a myth, and others hate your guts. But nevertheless, you're famous!" Aureum rambled, clearly dumbfounded.

Sabrina shrugged awkwardly, ignoring the weird feeling in her stomach. "Trust me, Aureum. No one knows me back home. I'm just your average human—er, mortal." She automatically corrected herself.

Aureum sighed and shook her head. "That's crazy. It's hard to believe, but you don't seem like the kind of person to lie. But, hey, here we are— Madam Rhea's room!" Aureum dropped their previous conversation, much to Sabrina's relief.

Sabrina looked at the fancy wooden door in front of her and took a shaky breath. She could do this.

"You ready?" Aureum asked with her hand on the doorknob.

Sabrina smiled weakly. "As ready as I'll ever be."

"You'll be fine, Sabrina. You've got this," Aureum assured her before twisting the doorknob to let them inside.

The girls walked into the classroom, and it reminded Sabrina of classrooms back at her home school. It was set up like the average chemistry classroom, with long tables meant for two people in rows. Aureum led

Sabrina to the front desk, where a lady with dark brown hair that was up in a messy bun was mixing potions together on her desk.

"Excuse me, Madam Rhea?" Aureum asked politely.

The lady looked up. Sabrina couldn't help but notice the multiple wrinkles from old age on her face. Her eyes were intense and seemed ancient, as if they had seen it all. But much to Sabrina's surprise, her eyes landed on Aureum, and she smiled warmly.

"Ah, Miss Cor, my prized pupil. What can I do for you? Oh and Miss Banner. I remember you from dinner last night. I must say, it is an honor to meet you." She came out from behind her desk to shake Sabrina's hand, and Sabrina gave her a small smile. "You're father was an excellent alchemist. You'd best hope his alchemy talent got passed down to you." Madam Rhea smiled at Sabrina.

Sabrina felt as if the weight of the world was pressing down on her.

She despised it.

Everyone expected her to be some hero.

Some goddess from a fairytale, a perfect student, a perfect *whatever.*

Sabrina realized that from that point on, almost everyone she would meet would have high expectations for her, and she feared that she wouldn't be able to meet the standards. They seemed to forget that she hadn't grown up here.

She was not like them.

She was different.

"Sabrina? Hello?" Sabrina blinked her eyes to find Aureum waving her hand in front of Sabrina's face.

Sabrina shook her head and snapped back to reality. "Oh, sorry. I was just … thinking," Sabrina partly lied.

Aureum rolled her eyes, but smiled in amusement. "I realized that, silly," she teased. "Now, come on!" She grabbed Sabrina's hand and led her to an empty desk, three desks away from the front.

The two sat down at a desk, Sabrina on the left and Aureum on the right.

"All right, class. Let's begin our lesson. Today you'll be creating a potion for making an object invisible. I kindly left the list of ingredients on a paper taped to the top of your desk. I wish you luck. You have until

the end of class to complete the task. And for those of you who are new ..."
Madam Rhea's eyes locked with Sabrina's eyes.

Sabrina squirmed a little in her seat, feeling under pressure.

"Each class lasts for an hour. Good luck, future alchemist. I expect nothing but the best from each of you—especially you, Miss Cor." Madam Rhea's called out Aureum, and Sabrina could see Aureum's cheeks heat up from embarrassment as she sank into her stool. "You may begin." Madam Rhea then returned to mixing potions that sat on her desk.

Aureum eyed the instructions that sat between them on the desk and read it to herself mumbling as she did so.

Sabrina looked down at the paper and found herself unable to read whatever was written on the paper.

It was like some new language that she'd never seen or heard of. Weird symbols decorated the page in what seemed to be no pattern. It made Sabrina's head hurt a little.

When Aureum was done, she let out a breath and said, "Okay, Sabrina. Can you read this paper or not?"

Heat rose to Sabrina's cheeks as she shook her head. "Sorry, but it looks a bunch of jumbled-up symbols and lines."

Aureum sighed. "This will be much more difficult now. But no matter! We'll prevail. Just listen to me, and I'll get you through this. I can teach you Bermuda later."

Sabrina frowned. *"Bermuda?"*

Aureum sighed again and waved her hand dismissively. "I'll explain later. Now, the first thing we need is a cauldron. They are over on the shelves behind Madam Rhea." Aureum pointed to where students were getting cauldrons on a shelf that sat behind Madam Rhea's desk.

"You can grab that while I gather other ingredients."

Sabrina nodded, and the girls parted ways. Sabrina went to grab a cauldron while Aureum collected some glass jars with ingredients in each of them from the other corner of the room. Sabrina forced herself to not gag when she saw eyes of some creature that she couldn't identify.

"Okay, to begin with, we need to pour this clear liquid into the cauldron." Aureum handed Sabrina an oddly shaped bottle.

"Um, do we pour all of it in?" Sabrina asked. Aureum nodded. Sabrina held her breath as she poured it into the cauldron, determined not to screw this up.

"Next, we add a small piece of ambrosia into it." Aureum held up a small golden square that slightly reminded Sabrina of fudge.

Then something in Sabrina's brain clicked, and she said, "Ambrosia, like the godly food used for healing wounds?"

Aureum shrugged. "A common misconception, but mostly, yes. Now I'll put this in." She held up an apple that was completely silver, and Sabrina's eyes widened in awe.

"A silver apple? Cool!" Sabrina watched it fall from her grasp into the cauldron.

The ingredients that were already in the cauldron turned the apple to acid and bubbled up.

"Next a small lock of unicorn hair." Aureum dropped a pink lock of hair into the cauldron. The liquid inside turned a midnight purple color and bubbles continued to form as steam rose. "Lastly, we put in some dragon eyes." She passed Sabrina the jar full of eyes that she had spotted earlier.

Sabrina once again forced down a wave of nausea that washed over her, her mind racing. *Unicorn hair?*

Dragon eyes?

Do those things really exist here?

It seemed so far-fetched, so unreal.

Sabrina started to pour the dragon eyes into the cauldron, her mind forgetting to ask Aureum how many should go in there. Aureum's attention wasn't on Sabrina as she read the instructions again. Aureum turned to face Sabrina and yelps as steam rapidly came up from the cauldron and bubbled rapidly formed.

"Oh, my gosh! Sabrina, you didn't wait for me to tell you to—"

She didn't get to finish because an explosion went off in the cauldron, causing black smoke to fill the room.

When it cleared, almost everyone had some black soot on them. Madame Rhea's glasses were completely covered with it, and Sabrina shrank down, trying to make herself as unnoticeable as possible and wishing that the invisibility potion would work on her.

"Miss Banner, Miss Cor, I expected more from you two," Madam

Rhea fumed. She snapped her fingers, and wind swept across the room When the wind stopped, the room was spotless.

Magical. Simply, magical.

"Madam Rhea, I'm so sorry. I didn't mean to cause the explosion! I couldn't read the instructions, and I didn't wait for Aureum's command. This is all my fault. If any of us have to get in trouble, it's me. I—"

Madam Rhea raised her hand to stop Sabrina's rambling.

The tips of Sabrina's ears turned pink, and she bit her tongue to keep her oversized mouth shut.

"Everyone makes mistakes, Miss Banner. But next time, be more careful. You're lucky that no one got hurt. I'm disappointed in you, Miss Cor. I have high expectations for you, especially considering who your father was. I hope you can change my thoughts about you by the end of the year—otherwise, it won't end very nicely."

The room fell into silence.

Sabrina nervously glanced over at Aureum, who looked like Sabrina, wanting to melt into the floor and hide from the embarrassment.

Aureum looked like she wanted to cry, and she looked so ashamed.

Ashamed of Sabrina mistake.

I'm a horrible friend, Sabrina thought sadly.

"I—I'll try harder next time, Madam Rhea," Aureum squeaked in a voice barely above a whisper. Sabrina wanted to comfort Aureum, to apologize for being such a screw up, but Aureum wouldn't even look at her. So much for making friends.

"You'd better. Now, I—" A loud bell went off, interrupting Madam Rhea.

She let out a huff of exasperation and ran a hand through her hair. "You're all dismissed to your next period class. I'm very disappointed." She turned her back to the students to organize papers.

The class slowly filed out of the room, with everyone but Aureum and Sabrina speaking in quiet whispers.

"Aureum, I'm so sorry. I didn't mean to, I—"

Aureum hugged her books closely to her chest and shook her head. "Please don't, Sabrina. Let's just get to our next class."

Sabrina felt her heart break a little as her shoulders slump in defeat.

"Yeah, okay," she replied glumly, her voice volume dropping to a whisper as well.

"What's your next period class?" Aureum asked quietly as they made their way down the hall. Sabrina exhaled deeply and said, "History, with Professor Linus."

They maneuvered their way through the crowded hallway.

"Okay, you have that class with Fern. I'll bring you there and then leave her to do the rest. All right?"

Sabrina nodded. "All right."

The rest of the way there was in silence, with guilt building up in Sabrina's stomach. Sabrina made a mental promise to herself that she'd make it up to Aureum.

Sabrina had a gut feeling that she had just ruined Aureum's good reputation. Being redeemed was easier said than done, but Sabrina would do it.

Now that Aureum was Sabrina's friend, Sabrina couldn't afford to lose her.

Not this quickly.

Sabrina became determined to find a way.

IV. "A Dark Past"

Sabrina exhaled deeply as she felt the awkwardness temporarily vanish as she and Aureum parted ways. Sabrina had tried to apologize to Aureum again because the guilty feeling was still there, but Aureum had brushed her off and told her to forget about it. Unfortunately for Sabrina, that made her want to apologize even more. Sabrina felt bad for embarrassing Aureum. Clearly, Aureum was one of Madam Rhea's prized pupils, and Sabrina had just embarrassed the girl, practically ruining Aureum's reputation in that class.

Sabrina hoped that a moment would come soon when she could redeem herself and make Aureum feel better. If it didn't, Sabrina was sure that the guilt was going to kill her before anything else did.

Sabrina let out another sigh as she entered the classroom for History with Professor Linus. It was the one lesson that she didn't have with Aureum but did have with Fern. When Sabrina walked inside, she noticed that it looked just like a classroom she would find back in the Mortal Realm.

Desks meant for one person instead of two were set up in rows, seven across and five down. There was a chalkboard in the front with the professor's desk off to the side. Almost all of the desks were filled in, like in alchemy class, but there was no teacher. Sabrina clutched the books that Amaris had given to her and walked farther into the room, looking for a spot to sit.

"Sabrina!" Sabrina glanced over in the direction from which she heard the voice and spotted Fern waving for her to come over.

Fern sat in the front row with a goofy smile on her face. Sabrina smiled, made her way over, plopped down in a seat beside Fern, and let out a breath of relief. "So what kind of stuff do we learn in this class?" she asked Fern.

"It's history class, Sabrina, so what do you think? We'd be learning the history of our realm, of course. And you've come on a great day! Yesterday, Professor Linus said he was going to take us on a trip to the—"

Before Fern could finish, the door to the room opened up, and a man in a walked into the room. He carried himself with pride, and his eyes traveled around the classroom, as if he had never been in it before. It was rather strange to Sabrina.

It gave her a weird feeling in her stomach, and something told her that she did not want to get on his bad side. "Hello, students." He sounded British, which made Sabrina question how sorcerers could develop accents similarly to those of the Mortal Realm. In her opinion, they should've been speaking some completely bizarre language that she'd never heard of, but here she was, able to understand them perfectly.

Sabrina shook her head, putting herself back into reality and ignoring the questions forming in her head. She needed to focus and learn.

This wasn't level one.

Amaris had bumped her up to match her with some of Fern and Aureum's levels because Amaris had claimed that she needed to learn as much as possible. With that being said, Sabrina needed to focus and take in everything that she was taught. She needed to stop questioning these things. Not to mention that it made her head hurt.

"As you may know, we have a new student in this class, but I'm sure you all heard who they are from last night, so I will not bother repeating it. In other news, we will be traveling around the Academy today and learning of those of whom we mustn't forget. From the villains who almost caused our extinction to those who made bold sacrifices to let us live. So without further ado, leave your books behind on the desks and follow me out of the classroom," the professor instructed.

His command was quickly carried out, much to Sabrina's surprise. She should just get used to things surprising her all the time, to be honest.

"Form a line, please, and remember to have a partner. No wandering off alone, no matter what. No touching the paintings on the walls or the objects behind the glass. You all know the rules, yet I still feel the need to repeat them. Do not finger the glass either; otherwise, you'll stay after to clean it, and I will not write you a pass to your next class. I hope I make myself clear. Now, come along."

Sabrina glanced over at Fern and whispered, "Jeez, that's a lot of rules."

Fern smiled faintly. "Professor Linus is very particular about how we act and what we do. One step out of line is a straight ticket to detention, so I'd mind his rules if I were you."

Sabrina nodded and the two picked up their pace to keep up with the rest of the class.

They rounded some corners and walked down some hallways. Sabrina knew that without the help up a map or a guide, she would never be able to find her way around the Academy.

Too many twists and turns.

Too much to remember.

"Ah, and here we are! Our first stop. This hallway is separate from your lockers and the other classrooms, due to the fact that we don't want these paintings to be ruined. They're rather priceless and keep alive the memory of the event and whom they represent," Professor Linus said. "Please be mindful and careful of the paintings. Do not touch them. I repeat for the millionth time, *do not touch them*. That means you, Owen."

Sabrina and Fern—along with the other students—turned around to see a boy with slicked back brown hair leaning over to touch a painting on the wall. The boy quickly recoiled from the painting and stuffed his hands into the pockets of his purple uniformed pants with a blush on his cheeks and a scowl on his face.

Professor Linus sighed before continuing on with his lesson. He turned around without another word and began to walk again. Sabrina gazed at the paintings in curiosity, while the other kids just ignored them as if they weren't of importance or the slightest bit interesting. It reminded Sabrina of how kids in her school back at home acted.

But considering that Sabrina had never been here before, it was all new and very intriguing to her. Sabrina didn't recognize any of the paintings that they passed, but Professor Linus didn't stop to discuss any of them.

Fern seemed to know some of them. She whispered to Sabrina about who some of the paintings were, but she stopped when Professor Linus began to speak.

"The main reason that we came here today was to discuss and see two things. One is this painting of an old student whom you all know much about." Professor Linus pointed to a painting of a man.

When Sabrina's eyes landed on it, she felt nothing.

No odd tension.

No recognition.

Nothing.

Sabrina was sure it would've sparked a memory of some sort.

Like in those movies where a character saw someone whom they hadn't seen in years but suddenly get a horrific flashback about the person.

But Sabrina didn't get anything.

Even though something told her that she should know the man in the painting that was before her.

But no memory sparked.

It was so strange.

"Sabrina, are you okay?" Fern whispered softly, placing a hand on Sabrina's shoulder.

"I, um …" Sabrina felt as though she couldn't use her voice.

There was something about this man—something not good—but Sabrina couldn't put her finger on it. Maybe it was a weird vibe that he gave. Maybe he was perfectly normal, and she was just being paranoid.

Maybe—

"Caspian Mare," Professor Linus began, cutting off Sabrina's train of thought with a grim expression on his face. "He was a wonderful student but had terrible intentions. Caspian wasn't in it for the ability to use magic and keep the realms in balance. No, he was in it for the power, as most villains are." Professor Linus sighed sadly.

Sabrina carefully studied the man in the painting.

She took in every detail because even though she felt no connection to the man, something in her gut told her to remember him. The man in the painting seemed frozen in time, as most people in paintings did. The man whom Professor Linus had called Caspian Mare had neatly kept black hair with one coal black eye.

One thing that struck Sabrina as odd was the scar that cut over his left eye, which resulted in that eye being blind. Caspian had his lips together in a thin line with a blank expression on his face. His perfect posture made him look ready to command an army, and he wore an all-black uniform.

Sabrina noticed the wrinkles on his face, under his eyes, and on his hands. Other than the scar on his left eye, he looked normal, not very villainous.

"He was a year away from graduating when his true colors began to show. Caspian wanted a way to travel between all of the realms, especially the Mortal Realm and the Sorcerer Realm. Caspian wanted a quest. He wanted permission to leave the Sorcerer Realm. The old Headmistress, Angelica Henry, wouldn't allow it. Mainly because it was forbidden for anyone, (not just Sorcerers) to have any contact with those from other realms unless a quest was granted. Not to mention that as you all know, Mortals think us to be a myth or a silly fantasy, and that's how it should stay."

Professor Linus let out a shaky breath before continuing.

"But eventually the time came that a quest was needed. Frederick Banner, Sylvester Coulson, Amaris Nightingale, and Caspian Mare were sent off on a quest in the Mortal Realm. While there, Fredrick broke the ancient rules and fell in love with a mortal, Aurora Noel. When they returned from their quest, shortly after, Frederick and Sylvester snuck back out of our realm again and went back to the Mortal Realm. Frederick caught up with Aurora, and their love grew even stronger than before. But Frederick and Sylvester knew they couldn't stay, and so after bidding the Mortal Realm a goodbye, they returned back to our realm. When Fredrick and Sylvester came back, little did they know that Aurora got pregnant and later gave birth to a baby girl."

Sabrina felt eyes fall onto her, and her body tensed up. Heat rose to her cheeks as she tried to avoid everyone's eyes. It made her uncomfortable.

"Caspian heard of their forbidden journey, and it sparked the idea that he too could travel between realms without a having to be granted a quest. He found it preposterous to not be able to go where he pleased, and that only certain people could receive a chance to travel realms. His anger, envy, and greed resulted in him fleeing to the Mortal Realm with the hopes of finding the last item to the ancient incantation to make it complete. He found Aurora Noel. It wasn't too hard, according to Sylvester. Frederick spoke highly of her, and believe it or not, Fredrrick and Caspian were good friends before Caspian turned. Caspian discovered her child and tried to take the child from Aurora. Aurora fled with her daughter, in fear of what Caspian had in mind." Professor Linus's eyes went to Sabrina, and Sabrina kept her gaze to the floor.

"Aurora went to her sister, Jeanette Clark, and gave the little half-blooded sorcerer to her to raise. Then Aurora ran off, only to be killed by Caspian's Nightshades. Caspian never found the child, fortunately enough, and the child grew up with her mortal family in the Mortal Realm, living blissfully unaware of our existence. Now we go to the present, where the child is with us. Miss Sabrina Banner."

There was a chorus of *oohs* and *aahs,* and Sabrina could've sworn that she looked like a tomato. Sabrina wanted to melt into the floor and disappear from their view. Of all of the things in history, why did the professor have to tell that story?

Coincidence?

I think not.

More like a convenient plotline, Sabrina thought in annoyance. On the bright side, at least know Sabrina now knew more about her father, Sylvester, and this Caspian guy.

"Any questions, class, before we move on to the last thing?"

A girl with curly brown hair and bright blue eyes quickly raised her hand. "Ooh! Me! Me, Professor!" Sabrina sucked in a breath, partly fearing the girl's question.

"Yes, Hazel?"

"The story you just told. It made sense and everything, but what about the prophecy?" Hazel said with a tilt of her head.

The professor smiled faintly. "Ah, the ancient prophecy. Miss Banner, I'm sure you can recite it for us?" He looked at Sabrina knowingly.

Sabrina scowled, hating him for putting her on the spot, but she obliged. She sucked in a breath before reciting the prophecy "*Born of mortal blood with magic in her veins, the daughter of a legend will soon begin her reign. She will journey far to seek what has been lost, but she will not return without a high cost. Betrayed by one she called friend, she will battle to the death, until the end.*"

Sabrina had only heard the prophecy twice, yet for some reason it flowed out of her, like it was something she had grown up knowing. It was as if it was a part of her—which it technically was.

"Thank you, Miss Banner. And to answer your question, Hazel, the prophecy was foretold almost a millennia ago by our prophet who is… no longer with us. The prophecy is very old indeed. But we know it to be happening soon, because of the arrival of Miss Sabrina Banner. The forbidden child and daughter of Frederick and Aurora Banner." Professor Linus smirked, although Sabrina couldn't tell why.

Did he enjoy putting her on the spot?

Did he not like her?

What had she done to him other than exist?

The other students in Sabrina's class continued to stare at her curiously. "Now, let's move on, shall we?" Professor Linus turned around and began to walk farther down the hall, past more portraits and strange items in showcases. Sabrina let out a breath of exasperation and followed after him, Fern by her side.

The class reached the end of the hallway to come face-to-face with a giant glass case containing a dark blue cloak that had a golden bottom trim and sparkled like the stars in the night sky. Professor Linus halted to a stop and turned around to face his students with his hands behind his back.

"This cloak belonged to the headmistress before Headmistress Amaris Nightingale. As you know, that would be Angelica Henry. She was killed in our great last battle, which I stated a few moments ago. Caspian intended on killing the headmistress himself to get what he wanted. With her out of the way, there would be less of a threat to keep him from getting what he wanted, and he succeeded. It was a horrible battle. But in her last living moments, Angelica temporarily postponed Caspian's plans and bought us some more time by cursing him and trapping him in the Mortal Realm"

Professor Linus reopened his eyes and longingly gazed at the cloak. "Angelica placed a protective shield around both realms to keep both realms safe and separate. That's where Caspian still lies among the mortals, making plans, finding allies, and searching for Frederick's child to complete his unfinished incantation. But now that Sabrina is here, I fear war will soon come, and he will come back stronger than ever before."

Professor Linus's voice was grim, and his expression was dark, sending shivers down Sabrina's spine. It gave her another reason to hate living.

If she hadn't existed, there would be no fear.

Her mom wouldn't have died.

Caspian wouldn't be a threat.

The prophecy would fail to come true.

Everyone would be safe.

Yet there she was, the forbidden prophecy child.

Sabrina's fate had been written in stone a millennia before she had even existed.

"All right, children. Follow me back to the classroom. The bell for next period will be ringing shortly, and I'm sure that none of you want to be late." Professor Linus began to lead the way back to down the hallway, and everyone else quietly and slowly trailed behind him.

Before Sabrina left, she got a weird feeling in the pit of her stomach. She shook it off and kept walking forward. Yet still something was almost compelling her to stay. She kept telling herself that she was paranoid and made herself continue to walk forward, ignoring the unsettling feeling in her stomach.

Sabrina caught up to Fern and the rest of the class, and thankfully Fern hadn't noticed her falling slightly behind. Sabrina suddenly felt a coldness sweep over her, and she froze in her tracks, letting everyone continue to walk in front of her. For some odd reason, her heart started to race a little, and she swallowed. The faintest sound of glass breaking made its way to her ears, causing her to spin around.

Sabrina glanced at the case that held the dead headmistress's cloak.

Nothing.

No crack in the glass.

That's it.

I'm finally losing it.

Reality is crashing down on me and reminding me that this is all one big hallucination.

No one else was aware that she had stopped, and they were a few feet ahead of her.

She heard the crackling sound again. What was going on?

She shook her head.

Just keep walking. Ignore the fact that you're probably going insane and keep up with the class, she told herself.

But the moment she started to move again, more glass cracking was heard.

No.

No.

Stop it.

Stop imagining this.

Sabrina wanted to scream or throw something, but she needed to keep her cool and act like everything was okay. She was simply tired.

Yeah, that had to be it.

But the crackling sound grew louder, causing the others to stop as well and turn toward the glass. Sabrina swallowed hard as she felt fear course through her.

"What the ...?" Professor Linus began, but before her could finish his sentence, the glass case around the cloak shattered into a million pieces, flying everywhere. Students screamed in terror. Some took cover on the floor, and others ran around in a panic.

A few like Sabrina simply covered their heads to avoid being hit by the glass.

Out of the blue, Sabrina's vision went black as a silky soft fabric covered her face and pushed her to the ground. She yelped in surprise and struggled to get the fabric off her face. When she finally managed to get peel it off, Sabrina realized that it was the cloak that had been trapped in the glass showcase. She held it in her fingertips and stared at it in awe and bewilderment, along with the others in her class.

No one spoke a word.

The cloak wiggled around in Sabrina's grasp as if it had a will of its own.

"What the heck is going on?" Sabrina screamed in terror.

"This, this is ... I can't ..." Professor Linus stammered in shock. He couldn't seem to fathom what had just happened. He ran a hand through his hair as he shakily rose to his feet. "My stars. I just ... You ... It chose *you*?" He finally managed to get out.

Sabrina made a face of pure confusion. "I'm sorry, but what? It *chose* me? It's a ... it's an inanimate object! How did it do that? That's it—I'm losing my mind! This is all a dream, and you're figments of my imagination!" Sabrina exclaimed, letting the cloak go from her fingertips as she paced around, running a hand through her hair. The outer space themed cloak didn't seem pleased with Sabrina releasing it from her grasp, and it flew back toward her, wrapping itself around her.

"What the—Hey, stop it!" Sabrina cried as she tried to take it off.

"Sabrina, wait! Calm down! It's okay!" Fern exclaimed as she got over her shock and ran over to assure Sabrina.

Sabrina's heart wouldn't stop hammering in her chest.

Sabrina stopped struggling to get the cloak off and noticed that the cloak had a tall, fancy collar and a golden chain that kept it clasped together around her neck. It was beautiful, Sabrina had to admit.

"It—it chose you," Professor Linus repeated again, though whether it was for himself or her, she couldn't tell.

"Care to elaborate, please?" Sabrina asked helplessly, desiring answers. She was tired of waiting for the answers to come. She needed to know.

Professor Linus let out a shaky breath before replying. "Like I said before, that cloak belonged to Angelica Henry. She was the headmistress of the Academy before Amaris took her position. After Angelica's death ..."

"But why did the cloak come to life and attack me?" Sabrina questioned, carefully choosing her words.

Professor Linus sighed and closed his eyes, as if remembering something or to recompose himself. "The cloak must've felt a connection with you, and it decided to move on from Angelica. Or maybe Angelica told it to wait until the prophecy child arrived. I'm not entirely sure. But every cloak is different. They are ... like us. They are alive, and some have attachment issues. But they don't feel pain or anything. It's hard to explain, and you wouldn't understand because this isn't normal for you. But long story short, the cloak is yours now. There's no getting rid of it," Professor Linus concluded.

Sabrina had so many more questions, but the professor seemed to have already dropped the subject. He turned back to face the rest of the class, who were recovering still from the surprise. "All right, class. Enough of this. The bell will be ringing shortly, and you all have lunch to attend to. I suggest that you hurry along. I will be informing Amaris of the incident, so you needn't worry. Come along now." With that, Professor Linus marched forward, and everyone slowly followed—except for Sabrina, who stayed frozen in her spot.

Fern remained next to her and quietly said, "Are you okay?"

Sabrina let out a shaky breath, managing to pull herself back together. "Y-yeah. I'll manage."

"You um, got a little cut on your upper lip." Fern noted, pointing to her own upper lip to indicate where the cut on Sabrina's lip was.

Sabrina's eyes widened in worried. "I do? Does it look bad? I didn't even notice that it happened. The glass must've done it. I must not have covered my face enough."

Fern cut off Sabrina's rambling. "Sabrina, chill. It's fine. Not too noticeable. Just on your bottom lip in the left corner. It'll heal, so just breathe. Now, we'd better get going or we'll be late to lunch." Fern grabbed Sabrina's hand and pulled her along, back to the dining hall.

Fern and Sabrina finally reached the lunch room, but not without getting stares of confusion when the students saw Angelica's cloak on Sabrina. Whispers could be heard in every direction, rumors were beginning to form, and Sabrina felt anxiety rise in her stomach. Sabrina wanted the day to end.

This is absolute madness!

But despite that, at least she could finally get some food. She hadn't realized how hungry she was. After all, she'd had a very eventful morning.

Sabrina noticed Angelica's cloak—or, her cloak now—was flowing elegantly behind her with every step she took, as if on command. Sabrina decided to ignore it and acted as if nothing out of the normal was happening. Then again, she didn't have much of anything to call normal anymore. Not since Sylvester whisked her away to this new world.

"Hey, Sabrina, slow down. What's wrong?" Fern asked from beside Sabrina, noticing the anxiety that Sabrina had been trying to hide.

As the two approach their table, Sabrina could see Aureum waiting for them. Sabrina shook her head and said, "It's nothing, Fern, really. I just don't like the weird looks everyone's giving me. First I'm the forbidden prophecy child, and next thing I know, the old, dead headmistress's cape—"

"Cloak," Fern corrected.

Sabrina nodded in appreciation. "Right. The cloak chose me to be its …"

"Master?" Fern offered.

"Yeah, master. Doesn't this all seem coincidental to you? Like it was planned out? Like a story, or a movie of sorts?" Sabrina questioned.

Fern shrugged. "Maybe? I don't know. You're probably just overthinking everything. You've been through a lot within your first day here. I just think it's fate. But never mind that. Let's eat." She grinned, plopped down at the table, and beckoned Sabrina to sit down too.

Sabrina sighed and placed her head on the table, exhausted from the chaotic day that seemed to happen at breakneck speed. After cooling off for a moment, Sabrina lifted her head up and looked at Aureum, guilt eating her inside out.

"Aureum … I know you told me it was fine, but I need to say this anyway. I'm sorry about screwing up on the potion earlier. I should've listened to you. I should've been more cautious. Now I've made that teacher not like you, and I've practically ruined your good reputation. I get it if you're mad, and you have every right to be mad. I also get it if you don't want to hang around me anymore. I'm so sorry. I just—"

"Hey. The apology is sweet, but please, just stop," Aureum interjected.

Fern sat there quietly, listening to the conversation but letting the two girls sort things out. Sabrina appreciated it.

Aureum continued. "It's okay, Sabrina. I'm simply not use to being frowned upon or called out for a mistake. I don't mean to make myself sound like a know-it-all or a snob, but it was something new for me. And I really love that class, so it just startled me. But it's all right. I'm over it. No need for you to apologize." Aureum gave a warm smile.

Sabrina still didn't feel any better about the situation. "But—"

Before Sabrina could protest anymore, Amaris stood up from the teacher's table and tapped her spoon against her glass goblet. "Students, I have one announcement before you can eat your lunch. I have been informed by Professor Linus of an … incident that happens moments before. Some of you have noticed that Sabrina is wearing Angelica's cloak. Sabrina did not break into the showcase and steal the cloak. Please be aware that according to Professor Linus, the cloak chose her. You all know how it works with cloaks: the cloak chooses its master, not the other way around. The rest of you who arrived last night will still be a part of the cloak choosing ceremony later this evening. That is all. Now, without further ado, you can enjoy your meal!"

V. "A Forbidden Quest"

Fern knew that Sabrina felt beyond grateful when they finally left the lunchroom.

Fern could only imagine what was going through Sabrina's mind as the three of them made their way to their next lesson. They were now on the way to one of Fern's favorite classes, Magic Defense with Professor Angus. Fern led the way to the class, and Aureum didn't seem to mind; she stayed back and walked beside Sabrina. The walk to their next lesson was quiet, but Fern was all right with it.

Normally, she couldn't stand the silence and would always feel the need to fill it in with something, but she let it slide, knowing that Sabrina probably needed it. Fern had many questions about Sabrina and her past, but she knew that now wasn't the right time to ask. Not after all that had just happened.

Because Sabrina was her roommate, Fern was sure that she would eventually learn more about the half-blooded sorceress. Fern wanted to know whether Sabrina was capable of stopping *the* Caspian Mare.

It seemed so far-fetched, but Fern refused to lose hope.

Sure, Sabrina knew nothing about being a sorcerer, but Fern was positive that Amaris had a plan. Or at least, she hoped that Amaris did. Fern shook her head and let herself smile as the trio approached their destination.

A wooden door with golden decorations that matched almost every other door in the Academy stood before them and would lead to Professor Angus.

"Are you ready?" Fern asked with excitement as she put her hand on the doorknob. She was grinning ear to ear. This was normal for her, and she loved this class even if she wasn't the best at it.

"As ready as I'll ever be," Sabrina responded with a small smile.

"Great! Let's go!" Fern cheered as she turned the doorknob. Aureum watched quietly as Fern pushed the door open to reveal a breathtaking courtyard, where their Magic Defense lesson would commence.

Fern adored the courtyard, which was one of her favorite places in the school. It was absolutely beautiful with its golden fountain in the center and tons bushes with flowers that decorated the rim. A big stone wall enclosed the courtyard, forming the courtyard into a triangular shape.

"Come on, Aureum and Sabrina! What are you waiting for?" Fern encouraged her friends as she walked into the courtyard. Sabrina and Aureum followed, both not meeting her enthusiasm but both still intrigued and ready to learn.

Fern continued to lead the way farther into the courtyard and around the fountain to where a bunch of other students stood, waiting for their instructor. Fern loved every minute of this class.

"Hurry up, you two!" Fern giggled excitedly, earning odd looks from other students as she made her way to the front of the crowd.

Eventually Professor Angus came into view, talking with one of the other students that Fern recognized to be Hazel, another good friend of hers. Sabrina and Aureum finally caught up with Fern, and the trio stood up in the front of the crowd of students, ready to begin.

"So this is Magic Defense, right?" Sabrina asked, wanting a confirmation.

Fern nodded. "Yep! And that's Professor Angus over there." She pointed to the professor, who had curly brown hair and was slightly bigger than most. He wore a purple suit like the other boys at the Academy with an orange-colored cloak following behind him.

"Hello children!" Professor Angus beamed, and Fern squealed happily as she grabbed Sabrina's arm to hopefully help contain her excitement.

"Hello Professor Angus," the class echoed back, except for Sabrina, who watched with interest.

"I hope that you're all as excited as I am to do some magic defense today! Especially you, Miss Banner!" Professor Angus pointed at Sabrina, and Fern noticed Sabrina shrink back a little. "You probably think this is all easy and fun, but it's not. It's hard work! Most have to work their way up to reach this level, but because you're supposed to save the world, Amaris let you cheat and move up the levels without learning the basics! I don't know how your other teachers have been handling this, but know that I won't go easy on you!"

This wasn't how Professor Angus normally was.

He never called anyone out like that, and it made Fern a little mad at him. She saw Sabrina shift uncomfortably on her feet and avoid his gaze, along with all of the other students who were now watching with interest.

"Anyway, at least Angelica's cloak is being used. I advise you to not misuse it or betray it. If you do, things will not end well for you," Professor Angus chided.

"Yes, sir," Sabrina replied quietly, looking embarrassed at being called out.

That made Fern sympatric for Sabrina.

"All right, everyone. I want you to stand in rows. Ten across, three down. Coincidently, we now have an even group of students, so please put yourselves in that position as quickly as possible because we have much to learn in very little time," Professor Angus commanded.

Students scattered about, talking loudly, pushing, and shoving as they tried to get into formation.

Fern ended up having Aureum on her left and Hazel on her right, Sabrina was a row in front of her next to Nicholas Nightingale. Fern cringed.

She hoped that Sabrina could put up with Nick.

He wasn't a fun person to be stuck next to.

Fern saw Nick turn to talk to Sabrina and say, "Aren't you that new girl? Sarah?"

Fern scrunched up her face in disgust.

Nick was so annoying.

"No, it's not Sarah. It's *Sabrina*," Sabrina sassed, and Fern smiled in approval.

"Oh, well, I—" Nick began, but Professor Angus cut him off, and Fern couldn't be more grateful.

"Students, pipe down! It's time for the less to start. Everyone, copy my movements and positions. Imagine a ball of energy forming at your fingertips. Feel at one with all of the realms. Breathe calmly in and out. Feel at peace." Professor Angus closed his eyes, outstretched his left hand, and began slow movements with his body.

He hummed simple notes as he moved, appearing completely at ease and relaxed. It seemed to be doing some sort of rehearsed dance routine and his body as he moved gracefully. He began to mumble words under his breath, as if chanting some old spells.

Fern had seen him do it many times before, but she still watched in awe at his elegance and concentration.

After a minute or so, a little purple flame sparked in the palm of his hand and danced across his fingertips. It was so mesmerizing and incredible, in Fern's opinion.

Professor Angus let the little flame dance across his fingertips without being burned or harmed.

Fern glanced over at Aureum, who stood staring calmly at him.

Fern slightly envied Aureum for always acting calm and getting every new challenge correct.

Aureum was very wise and a quick learner. Fern wished she could relate to that.

Determination was evident on Aureum's face, as though she was ready to master this technique, which wouldn't surprise Fern the slightest.

Finally, Professor Angus stopped moving and placed his hands together. He mumbled words under his breath.

Professor Angus opened his eyes and slowly pulled his hands apart, each holding a ball of burning fire.

Fern's eyes widened, and her jaw dropped. She hadn't seen him do this before. Fern momentarily wondered how Sabrina was taking it all in.

Professor Angus abruptly interrupts Fern's thoughts. "Okay, students. Now it's your turn. Repeat my moves slowly, and if done right, you should all have a flame in your hand. If you get one, excellent! If you get two, then you're an overachiever! You'll get the hang of it. Trust me. Simply focus on finding your inner peace." He said, trying to soothe his students.

Everyone else was anxious to begin. Professor Angus awkwardly cleared his throat and fixed his feet position. "All right, begin with your feet like this ..."

Time flew by as sweat trickled down the side of Fern's face.

She tried so hard, but she couldn't seem to master what Professor Angus was doing. A few people had managed to make a ball of fire, but Fern, Aureum, Sabrina, and Hazel had not accomplished it. Then as if on cue, Hazel suddenly cheered, "Ah-ha! I did it!" She beamed with one hand holding a ball of fire.

"Good job, Hazel. Now try for a second one. Everyone else, keep working at it. We'll do this for a little bit longer before we switch to some more physical activities," Professor Angus informed his students. Sabrina let out a shaky breath and closed her eyes.

Just a few more minutes to get this down.

Come on, Fern!

You can do this!

Just focus! Fern mentally encouraged herself.

Fern's eyes were shut, and she practiced the movements from memory. She felt herself getting more frustrated by the second. Fern wasn't normally a fast learner, but in this class, she usually did very well.

"I—I did it! Fern, look, I did it!" Aureum happily cried. Fern inwardly groaned as her concentration broke, and she opened her eyes to see Aureum holding a ball of fire in one hand and a ball of fire in the other.

"Remarkable! Well done, Miss Cor! All right kids, stop trying the ball of flame. Now we're going to move onto some physical activities," Professor Angus said with a grin, causing the whole class to groan.

Soon enough the lesson came to an end, and everyone was exhausted.

The students dispersed from the courtyard and headed back into the Academy to make it to the dining hall for dinner.

Fern couldn't wait to eat because she was starving.

Sure, they had only had one class after lunch, but this class was the longest. They had two lessons after breakfast, and one after lunch, and sometimes additional lessons after dinner.

As Fern, Aureum, and Sabrina sat in the dining hall at their normal table, Fern noticed Sabrina admiring the Academy. Fern couldn't blame Sabrina from doing so. After all, the Academy was quiet beautiful. Sabrina sighed and placed her head on the table edge.

"Tired Sabrina?" Aureum asked before Fern could.

Sabrina exhaled in response and grumbled, "Potato."

Aureum laughed softly. "Figures. Being a sorcerer is not easy."

"Yeah, no kidding," Sabrina mumbled in agreement.

Fern bit her tongue keep herself from saying anything about how Aureum shouldn't complain about being tired because of how easily she mastered everything. It wasn't fair. Fern decided to speak to distract herself from her thoughts. "I can't wait to eat!"

Sabrina lifted her head off of the table as Aureum spoke, "The headmistress still has to give her nightly speech."

Fern nodded. "I know, but I'm starving. I already know what I'm going to have tonight, and I can almost taste it in my mouth."

Aureum rolled her eyes, but she had the faintest smile on her lips.

Much to Fern's relief, Amaris stood up from her spot at the teacher table.

"Good evening, students! I hope you all had a wonderful day at the Academy and have learned much about yourself as well as mastered some new powers. Now you're all free to eat. Enjoy your meals!"

Amaris smiles and everyone cheered.

She sat back down, and in the blink of an eye, food appeared on students' plates. On Fern's plate, a big salad appeared

Sabrina laughed. "You've been waiting all this time for a *salad?*" she teased.

Fern glared at her playfully before they both started laughing. "You're hilarious, Sabrina, *really.*"

Sabrina smirked cockily and replied, "Yeah, I know."

The rest of dinner went by quickly.

Fern and Sabrina soon retired to their dorms for the night, and Fern had never been happier to go to sleep. Fern learned that Sabrina hadn't been able to master anything that Professor Angus had taught that day and was frustrated. Fern assured her that she'd get the hang of it eventually and that Aureum could probably help her in her spare time.

Sabrina thanked Fern for the idea, and the two of them headed off to bed.

Sabrina ended up taking a quick shower before tossing on a pair of pajamas and snuggled into bed.

As for Fern, she was already in bed, waiting to fall asleep.

Fern was abruptly awoken during the night by heavy footsteps entering the dorm.

She lay in bed not making a sound and trying to figure out who the intruder was. She kept her eyes closed as she turned herself over. She was facing Sabrina's bed and prayed that the intruder thought she was sleeping. Fern slowly opened her eyelids enough so that she could see, but not enough for it to look like she was awake.

A figure of a man stood with his back turned to her and facing Sabrina.

This was creepy and beyond weird.

Fern studied the man's appearance to see if anything about the man struck a memory.

The man wore a trench coat, but Fern couldn't say what color it was in the dark. Fern noticed Sabrina stir in her sleep and prayed that Sabrina would wake up. Fern watched as the man suddenly placed a hand on Sabrina's shoulder and gently shook Sabrina awake. Sabrina groaned, and her eyes started to open.

"Fern?" she called out sleepily.

Fern wanted to spring out of bed and tell Sabrina to run, but she found herself frozen in place and unable to do anything but watch.

The man quickly outstretched his hand toward Sabrina's sleeping figure, and he covered Sabrina's mouth with his hand as if trying to keep Sabrina quiet.

"Gross! Did you just lick my hand?" the man cried, jumping back from Sabrina, who was now sitting up and fully awake. His voice seemed oddly familiar to Fern, but she just put her finger on it.

Fortunately, Sabrina recognized the man and said, "Sylvester? What are you doing here?"

Fern's body seemed to work again, and she forced her tired self to sit up in bed, looking at the man before her. "We don't have much time, Sabrina. Change into a pair of clothes and meet me in the hallway. We have important matters to attend to in the Mortal Realm," Sylvester explained in a hushed voice. "What's going on? What are you doing in our room?" Fern demanded, earning Sylvester and Sabrina's full attention.

"Oh, um, well, you see, it's rather complicated," Sylvester stammered sheepishly.

"Can I just sleep? *Please?*" Sabrina complained.

Fern's question went unanswered, and she rubbed her eyes.

"No can do, Sabrina. If you ever wish to return home, then you need to cooperate. Now, get dressed, we have places to be. Five minutes—go!" Sylvester exclaimed.

Sabrina rolled out of bed and almost fell onto the floor, but she managed to catch herself.

"Wait. Sabrina, you're just going to trust that guy just like that? What the heck is going on?" Fern cried in bewilderment.

Sabrina sighed, pinched the bridge of her nose, and shook her head. "Believe me, I wish I knew. But I've got to see what Sylvester wants. I'll be back soon and will tell you everything, all right?" Sabrina pried open the trunk at the end of her bed and pulled out a fresh uniform.

"Yeah, okay," Fern agreed, unease evident in her voice.

Sabrina ran a hand through her short and curly blonde hair again before heading into the bathroom to change.

When Sabrina comes out, she is dressed in a fresh school uniform and lets Sylvester into the room. "Okay, so, Sylvester, care to explain why you're here and why I have to be dressed and ready to leave a five o'clock in the morning?" Sabrina asks with her arms crossed.

"I believe that I know of a way to find your father and Caspian," Sylvester says slowly.

Fern blinked in confusion. "Care to elaborate? I'm a little lost." Sabrina nods in agreement. "Same. I'm completely confused. My Dad is dead, isn't he? How could we find someone who is dead?"

Sylvester exhaled deeply and quickly said, "Allow me to explain. Long story short, Caspian was after Sabrina's father because after he learned of Sabrina's existence, he decided that if he found Fred he could find Sabrina. This would result in him getting the final ingredient to cast the spell that would break Angelica Henry's curse that keeps his soul bounded to the Mortal Realm." "Wait, *ingredient?*" Sabrina questioned, knitting her eyebrows together in confusion. "When Angelica casted her curse, the only way to break it was if Caspian collected certain ingredients to cast an ancient spell to counteract her curse." Fern chimed in.

Sabrina nodded slowly, taking it all in.

"This is crazy and seems really risky," she remarked. "So you're saying that Caspian has had my father held as a prisoner to try and find me?"

Sylvester shifted awkwardly on his feet as he nodded in confirm nation. "I know its risky Sabrina, but I just can't pass up this opportunity. Please don't tell Amaris."

Fern and Sabrina shared a look before Sabrina let out a sigh. "All right, Sylvester. We won't tell Amaris. But how can you be sure that you get back safely? You could be walking straight into a trap and Sabrina is an inexperienced sorceress. I would offer to go, but I need to focus on my studies." Fern notes.

"She has a point." Sabrina agrees and Sylvester frowns in thought.

Sabrina then purses her lips as the trio sit in silence, contemplating on what to do. Then as if a light bulb had gone off in her head, Sabrina's eyes lit up. "Aureum!" Sabrina exclaimed. Sylvester looked at her in confusion. "Who?"

"Aureum Cor. She can help us. I mean, Fern, you saw her in Magic Defense class. She's clearly a very skilled sorcerer and knows how to use potions and magic. Maybe we can convince her to come." Sabrina replies with excitement. Fern nods slowly, considering Sabrina's idea. "She might agree to go…But then again she's very focused on her studies, like me. I don't see how you'll get Aureum to go along. You're breaking one of the biggest rules, and that's not what Aureum does. Also, you need a realm traveling device, and those aren't just handed out to anyone. Only professors get them, and people who've gone on quests. But even after the quest, the device is taken away." Fern deadpans.

"True…" Sylvester hums aloud in thought then he gasps as an idea comes to mind. "Wait, did you say that her last name is, '*Cor*'?"

"Yeah, so?" Fern questions.

"I knew her father when he…never mind that. I know how to convince her to join us." He responds. Sabrina scrunches her nose up in puzzlement. "How?"

"I'll explain later Sabrina. You needn't worry!" Sylvester exclaimed.

Fern sighed again. "All right, if you say so. But since you're getting Aureum involved, I suppose that you'll need directions to Aureum's dorm?"

Sabrina grins sheepishly. "That would be nice …"

VI. "Aureum Knows All"

Aureum was having a peaceful sleep until she was abruptly awaken by someone knocking on her dorm door.

She groaned as she pushed the warm bed sheets off of her. Who on earth would be trying to wake her up at this hour?

Aureum trudged over to answer her door, rubbing the grogginess from her eyes. She yawned before twisting the doorknob and pulling the door open, only to be greeted by Fern, Sabrina, and some man whom she had never seen before.

"Sabrina? Fern? What's going on?" Aureum asked in confusion, still trying to wake up.

After all, it was only four in the morning—much too early to be out of bed, in her opinion. Sabrina rubbed the back of her neck.

"Well, um, you see—"

"No," Aureum deadpanned.

Sabrina's eyes widened in surprise. "But—but you don't even know what I was going to say!" she stammered, flabbergasted and confused.

Aureum sighed and crossed her arms. "I'm assuming that you want to do something that goes against the Academy rules, correct?"

"What? No, of course not." Sabrina chuckled awkwardly.

"Sabrina, you're terrible at lying. Now, if you don't mind, I'd like to go back to sleep, please," Aureum said, and she went to close her dorm door.

Sabrina stopped it with her foot. "Aureum, please! At least let me—er, *us*, explain."

Aureum sighed in defeat before opening up her door. "Well, come in then, I guess."

Sabrina smiled and quickly led the way inside, with Fern and the strange man in tow. "Thank you, Aureum. It really means a lot, and I—" she began.

Aureum cut her off. "Don't thank me yet, Sabrina. I haven't done anything yet. Now, please explain." Aureum sat down on her bed. At this moment, she felt grateful for not having a roommate. Otherwise, this might've played out differently.

"Oh um, right. But before I do, this is Sylvester. He's my dad's … best friend?" Sabrina offered, glancing over at the man, who nodded in confirmation. "Right. So, um, Sylvester was my dad's best friend, and my dad disappeared when I was little. I always thought that he was dead but turns out Sylvester claims that he was taken as a prisoner by Caspian and Sylvester knows where he is and how to get him back."

Aureum placed a hand to her head, slightly confused. "I don't understand. And Fern, why are you here?"

Fern shrugged. "I just had to show Sabrina the way here. Couldn't have her wandering the halls after curfew," she replied.

Aureum nodded slowly. "Right. Anyway, you want to go with... *Sylvester* and find your Dad?" Aureum said slowly, and Sabrina nodded. "I don't see how I play a part in this."

"Well, you're an extremely talented sorceress, according to Fern and what I saw in class today—way more advanced than me—and Sylvester is experienced, but we thought that it would be a good thing to have you along. Plus, we're going to the Mortal Realm, which is a place that you've always wanted to see, right?" Sabrina pressed with a knowing smile.

"Well, yeah, of course. But why can't you take Fern with you? I don't want to break any rules. We're not supposed to go on trips to the Mortal Realm without a quest," Aureum noted.

Sabrina said, "I know, Aureum. But Fern wants to stay back and work on her studies so I thought of you. Also this is probably my one shot to save at *least* one of my parents. My mom's gone, but I might be able to see my dad again. And I might even get a chance at stopping Caspian which would not just benefit me, but *everyone* else as well." Sabrina replied.

"Not to mention that I was friends with your father, Aureum," Sylvester chimed in, earning Aureum's full attention.

Aureum subconsciously clutched her belt with one hand. "My-my father?" she stammered.

Sylvester nodded. "Yes. Ingram Cor. A very wise man. You know what it's like to lose a parent, Aureum. If you had a chance to get your father back, wouldn't you take it?"

Aureum didn't hesitate to say, "Of course I would. But what does my father have to do with any of this?"

"Yeah, Sylvester. What does her father have to do with any of this?" Sabrina chirped, making Aureum even more confused.

Sylvester pointed to Aureum's belt and said, "That's what her father has to do with all of this. Ingram was one of the few people who was trusted with a Realm Traveling Device. So not only will you help us by having more experience with magic and potions, but you'll also be our ride between realms."

Aureum frowned. "B-but just because my dad had a Realm Traveling Device, what makes you think I have one?"

"Your belt, Aureum, was from your father, correct?" Sylvester asked, gesturing to the belt around Aureum's waist.

"Yeah …" Aureum agreed slowly.

Sabrina and Fern watched with curiosity, all three of the girls sharing the same confusion.

"Ingram's Realm Traveling Device, or RTD, was his belt in which he carried all of his potions."

"Wait, so for the past fifteen years of my life, I've been wearing an RTD without even knowing it?" Aureum screeched, not knowing how to feel about it. A worrisome thought suddenly came to her mind. *If RTDs are only given to certain people, to the worthy, by the Council of the Realms, then that means …*

"Oh, my gosh! I've been carrying this thing around illegally for like twelve years!" Aureum cried, cutting off her own internal dialogue in shock and slight fear.

"Apparently so," Sabrina answered.

"Wow. I just … Wow," Aureum murmured, feeling overwhelmed and also somewhat like a criminal.

"So will you help us, Aureum?" Sylvester asked. "For your dad, and for Sabrina's sake?"

Aureum glanced between the three people in front of her, struggling to make a choice. She wanted to make her dad proud, but she didn't want to break the rules. She let out a shaky breath and said, "All right, fine. I'll help you. Because I would know that I would kill to have my dad back."

Sabrina grinned and hugged Aureum tightly. "Thank you so much, Aureum!"

Aureum manages a smile and patted Sabrina on the back. "You're welcome, Sabrina. Now, Fern, are you coming along too?" she asked, turning to face her old friend.

Fern shook her head, waving her hands back and forth before saying, "No, no, no. I'm not ... prepared or trained enough for this. I'll stay back and cover you guys so that hopefully Amaris won't notice as quickly," she responded with a smile.

Aureum nodded. "Okay, if you say so. When do we leave?" Aureum asked, addressing Sylvester and Sabrina.

"Tonight. As soon as possible and before everyone wakes up. We're heading to Miami, Florida," Sylvester announced.

Sabrina furrowed her eyebrows and frowned. "Florida? Why Florida?"

"Because Florida is the near the—"

"Bermuda Triangle." Aureum filled in, surprising Sylvester.

"How did you ...?"

Aureum smiled and replied, "Don't underestimate my knowledge. I do my research."

"Well, that's good to know," Sylvester responded with a nod of approval.

"What does the Bermuda Triangle have to do with anything?" Sabrina exclaimed, not grasping the situation at hand.

Sylvester sighed in slight annoyance before responding with, "So you know how myths in your world refer to it as a place where things such as planes and ships go missing?"

"Yeah..." Sabrina's voice trailed off in acknowledgement.

"Well that's where Angelica trapped Caspian and that's where Caspian probably has your father." Aureum responded and Sabrina frowned.

"If Caspian is trapped there then how did he get my father? This isn't making any sense." "Caspian has these minions that he calls, Nightshades."

Fern chimed in. "He pulls magic from the Dark Realm to create them, making them considered to be, Monsters. Unlike him, they have the ability to Realm Travel and go outside of the Bermuda triangle, so they can do Caspian's dirty work."

"They're these creatures that look like shadows and can morph their shape to mimic anything that they want to. They can also possess people and choose whether or not to live with that person's soul or eat the soul and use the body at free will. They're bad news." Aureum concluded with a shiver and Sabrina cringed. "That does not sound like fun."

"Well of course not! But let's move on. Other than knowing your location, how long will guys be gone for?" Fern asked.

Sylvester hummed aloud while thinking before saying, "A week, at most. Maybe a bit less or a bit more. Hopefully less though, as long as it all goes well of course."

Sabrina let out a sigh of relief. "Good. Because I need to get back home within the next twelve days."

Aureum frowned. "How come? Don't you like it here?"

Sabrina nodded. "Of course I do! But I'm only on spring break for two weeks. If I'm not back soon, people will grow suspicious, and that won't do me any good."

"Oh. Well, I'm not really sure as to what *spring break* is, but I get it," Aureum said.

Sabrina pushes the subject aside. "I'll explain it to you some other time. We have work to do."

"Right. We need to pack," Aureum agreed, getting back on track.

"*Pack?*" Sylvester repeated, titling his head in confusion.

"Yes, *pack.*" Aureum turned around and frowned.

"You seriously didn't plan on winging this whole thing, did you?" Sylvester grinned sheepishly.

Sabrina gasped in surprise. "I thought you had a plan!" she exclaimed.

Sylvester shrugged. "Well, I have a mostly thought-out plan, but packing didn't cross my mind."

"My God. Good thing we have Aureum to help us now," Sabrina mumbled, shaking her head.

Aureum sighed and took on the leader role. "Sylvester, I assume that you didn't bring any bags, food, clothes, or a first aid kit with you. Sabrina, can you head back to your room and pack a bag? Meet back here at my dorm in ten minutes. It's almost five thirty. We've got about an hour to make sure that other students don't wake up early and try to stop us."

Sabrina nodded. "Sounds like a good idea."

The group split up.

Fern, Sabrina, and Sylvester headed off to pack, leaving Aureum by herself. Aureum packed up a small bag with possible needed essentials. A few minutes later, Sabrina and Sylvester (this time without Fern) arrived packed and ready to go. Aureum ended up braiding her long brown hair over her shoulder to keep it out of her face for traveling.

"You ready?" Sabrina asked Aureum as she stepped out of her dorm and tucked her keys into a pocket of her belt.

Aureum sucked in a breath and nodded stiffly. "As I'll ever be. Mr. Coulson, are you coming?" she asked politely. She glanced back to her dorm to see Sylvester making his way toward them with a backpack. Aureum assumed that Sabrina or Fern had lent him one.

"Yes, I believe I am ready. And please, Aureum, no need to be so formal. Just Sylvester will do."

Aureum flushed slightly from embarrassment but nodded.

"So ..." Sabrina began.

Aureum remembered something and cut her off. "Wait! I forgot something in my dorm. I'll be back in a second!" She disappeared into her dorm and reappeared a second later with a little baby chick on her shoulder.

Sabrina frowned. "Aureum, why do you have a chicken ... with, horns?" she asked.

Aureum smiled and said, "This is Chi, my pet. Since we're going to be gone for a while, I couldn't just leave him in my dorm by himself without someone to take care of him, so he's coming with us," she declared.

"Okay, then." Sabrina awkwardly cleared her throat. "Anyway, do you have any idea as to how Ingram used the belt to realm travel?"

Aureum glanced down at the belt, and her lips turn downward into a frown. She hummed aloud in thought. "I have no idea as to how it works," she finally admitted, and she pressed her lips together. "There are buttons on it, and random gears. Maybe one of them is what does it?" Aureum hated feeling so helpless.

"Maybe ..." Sylvester pondered, scratching his chin in thought. "Do you have any family members who might have known how Ingram used the belt? Maybe his wife, Tara Cor? Or a sibling?"

"My mom might know, but she'd be suspicious if we went into town and randomly asked her how to use the belt. She wouldn't tell us. Despite the fact that I'm her daughter, she never told me about the belt. She would want to know how I know about it and why I need to use it. Then if she found out we were breaking ancient rules and traveling to the Mortal Realm, she'd probably take the belt from me."

Sylvester snapped his fingers and exclaimed, "Jerry! Jerry would know how it works! He's the one who made it, I think. And even if he didn't, he makes other RTDs for sorcerers who go on quests to other realms. Surely he'd know how it works!" Then Sylvester's smile dropped, and his shoulders slumped as he shook his head. "Actually, never mind. Jerry won't help either. I had to borrow a RTD from him to bring Sabrina here. After that, he probably won't ever lend me one again, and he's terrible at keeping secrets."

Sylvester crossed his arms and let out a huff of annoyance.

The trio stood in silence, at a loss and not sure how to work Aureum's belt.

Then Sabrina's head perked up when she heard the distant sound of high heels clamping against the concrete floor. "Anyone else here wearing high heels?" Sabrina asked, breaking the silence.

Sylvester's face became grim.

Aureum said, "It's Amaris. I recognize the sound. She's probably going around and making sure students are in their dorms." Sabrina pales slightly, and Aureum feels herself freeze up with fear. She didn't want to get caught, especially not by the headmistress herself.

This could end badly if they didn't act quickly.

Aureum didn't need to lose Amaris's trust, and neither did Sabrina, but Aureum knew that Sabrina needed to do this. They needed to find out how to work Aureum's belt before Amaris saw it.

Aureum began to panic even more, as the footsteps came closer. Sylvester looked like he was panicking too as he fiddled with random buttons and switches on Aureum's belt. "Can't you go any faster? Amaris is almost here!" Sabrina exclaimed frantically.

Aureum felt ready to break down and cry. "We need to hurry! I can't ruin my reputation any more than it's already ruined! I can't get in trouble. Please hurry!" she pleaded. She didn't want to get into trouble.

"Sylvester? Sabrina? Aureum? What are you doing?" Amaris's shocked voice came from behind them. Aureum glanced over her shoulder to see Amaris staring back at them in horror.

"Amaris, I'm sorry. I'll explain everything when we get back. I promise!" Sabrina called to her. Aureum could hear the guilt in Sabrina's voice.

"Ah-ha! I found it, I think … Oh, well! I'm hitting it! Sabrina, grab onto Aureum's arm!" Sylvester commanded urgently.

Sabrina quickly obliged and grasped Aureum's arm. Aureum caught a glimpse of Amaris's face: the betrayal and confusion evident did not make her feel any better. Sylvester pressed a button on Aureum's belt, and Aureum squeezed her eyes shut, preparing herself for the worst. She wasn't sure whether she had screamed, but the next thing she knew, a wave of freezing cold washed over her, and her world went temporarily black.

Aureum's vision came into focus, and when it did, she discovered herself lying on a sandy beach. Aureum sat up, feeling slightly nauseous. She'd never realm traveled before.

"Oh, good! Aureum, you're awake!" Sylvester exclaimed, letting out a sigh of relief. "You can help me wake up Sabrina."

Aureum glanced over to where Sylvester was pointing and saw Sabrina passed out in the sand. "Sabrina? Come on, Sabrina. You need to wake up," Sylvester repeated, shaking the sleeping girl back and forth.

Aureum watched Sylvester try to wake up Sabrina. Sabrina groaned and groggily woke up. She looked so drained and exhausted. "Sylvester?" Sabrina grumbled, rubbing her eyes with her hand as she pushed herself up into a sitting position. "What … what happened? Where are we?"

"Welcome back to the Mortal Realm, Sabrina. You've been out for a few hours. Aureum and I tried to wake you, but no such luck. You could probably sleep through a tornado."

Sylvester shook his head and helped Sabrina up to her feet.

Aureum took this as her cue to stand up as well.

"Ugh, my head hurts. Um, why are we on a beach?" Sabrina mumbled, still trying to wake herself up.

"It's where we landed," Sylvester quickly explained. "Realm traveling doesn't always get you to your exact intended location. Magic can't do everything, y'know. I woke up before you two, and then Aureum followed soon after. After I made sure that she was okay, I woke you up. We should start heading toward the Bermuda, where Caspian is. The tide will be coming in soon, so now that you're awake, we need to pack up and start moving."

"Wait, what time is it?" Aureum asked as she brushed sand off of her purple skirt, and Sabrina ran a hand through her hair in bewilderment.

Sylvester glanced down at his wrist watch and replied, "Five thirty-two in the evening. We've all been out for a while. Aureum, are you ready to go?"

Aureum repacked backpack. "Yeah, just give me a second. And hey, we should probably put our cloaks in our backpacks. It'll look strange if mortals see us walking around and wearing them."

Sylvester nodded in agreement. "Good call, Aureum. Let's put our cloaks away, and then we'll move out!" He took off his backpack and began to take off his cloak. Sabrina obliged and put her cloak away too. Then the trio came together before they headed off of the beach and onto an almost abandoned, sandy boardwalk.

"Where are we? Where are going? Do you even know where Caspian's headquarters is?" Sabrina blurted.

"We are nearing the Bermuda Triangle and like I said before we left, if I know anything, that's where Angelica trapped Caspian. Knowing him, he's set up his base somewhere along the magical barrier of the Sorcerer Realm."

Aureum broke into a jog so that she could catch up with Sabrina and Sylvester. They walked past shops, cafés, and rentable apartment buildings to stay in for a vacation place. *This place is pretty cool*, Aureum thought, admiring everything about the Mortal Realm. If they had more time, she would gladly stay here longer and enjoy the Mortal Realm and the beach that she had read so much about.

"Sylvester, this is so confusing. I mean, I know where we're going but do you know how long it could take us to pinpoint Caspian's exact location in the Bermuda triangle?" Sabrina said in a matter-of-fact voice as they maneuvered their way through the crowded sidewalks and crossed the street to a bus stop.

"I can't explain it to you Sabrina, but I know where we are going and how to get there. Trust me. Besides, the Sorcerer Realm has Peacekeepers who keep an eye on Caspian's whereabouts. They may not be able to exactly 'pinpoint' where he is, but they do have a rough idea. And they release it to the public every once and a while to keep panic down to a minimum. So trust me. I want your father back as much as you do. I know what we're doing." Sylvester was dead serious.

Sabrina kept her mouth shut for the rest of the walk, as did Aureum.

Aureum ignored the uneasy feeling in her stomach, despite the fact that her instincts were telling her to run.

VII. "In Which Sabrina Meets a Chick Named Chi"

Aureum adjusted the backpack on her shoulders as they waited at a bus stop.

Chi sat on Aureum's shoulder, sleeping peacefully. Aureum wished that she could take a nap as well, but now wasn't the time. Aureum also wished she knew more about what was going on and wished that she could trust Sylvester but something in her gut told her not to. Even though she knew where they were going where going, Aureum still couldn't help but question Sylvester's tactics.

This was especially due to the fact that he was acting so anxious and antsy.

It made Aureum feel uneasy, and it was a little nerve-wracking. From the moment Aureum had met Sylvester, he has seemed like a calm, easygoing guy who went wherever the wind took him. But now they seemed to be under some time limit because Sylvester kept checking his wrist watch every five seconds and nervously glancing over his shoulder, as if someone or something was following them.

It didn't calm Aureum's nerves or make her feel very safe, and based upon Sabrina's anxious fidgeting, she would agree with Aureum on that.

Sylvester tapped his foot against the pavement with his arms crossed over his chest. It was like they were on a time schedule, but as far as Aureum knew, their only time schedule was getting Sabrina back for her mortal school before her break was over.

According to Sabrina, they had a total of ten days to do so. She didn't know what had Sylvester so on edge, but maybe this was Sylvester's normal.

After all, she had only known him for a couple of hours.

Aureum glanced over at Sabrina, who looked worried and deep in thought.

Aureum couldn't imagine how Sabrina must be feeling. She had the weight of the world, and all of the realms, on her shoulders.

Aureum's home and millions of other homes depended on Sabrina's actions and choices. She hoped that Sabrina knew what she was doing and that Sabrina had made the right choice by bringing along Aureum. She didn't want to think about it anymore.

The mere thought of the realms crumbling made adrenaline pump through her veins. It made her scared—no, terrified. If Sabrina made one wrong step, everything would come crashing down. The realms would collide. People would die. And everything would turn to chaos. All hell would break loose, and Caspian would win.

Aureum shivered at the thought.

Even if it was a little selfish, she couldn't help but be grateful that she wasn't the prophecy child. She wouldn't have been able to handle the pressure. She had to give Sabrina credit for that much.

Aureum sighed as she looked over at the road before them.

This was all very strange.

Sure, she had learned about the Mortal Realm and was very fascinated by it, but it still scared her. Aureum was completely out of her comfort zone and they couldn't let the mortals know of their presence. It would cause so much chaos. That was why their worlds stayed separate.

Sorcerers were more advanced and could understand things that mortals couldn't. If normal mortals went to the Sorcerer Realm, it would drive them insane in a matter of seconds. Aureum wished that it wasn't case because she would love to tour the Mortal Realm. It was so interesting and safe.

There was no constant threat of magic beasts, or the fear of a rip in the realms.

What Aureum wouldn't give to be mortal and to live blissfully unaware of the realms. It's something she slightly envied about Sabrina. Sabrina got both the magic and the normality. Even though she did enjoy magic and the knowledge that came with being a sorcerer, it would be a nice getaway.

"Ooh! Here comes the bus!" Sylvester beamed, snapping Aureum out of her thoughts.

Aureum couldn't help but mentally wonder what a weird word *bus* was. She had learned about them, of course, from countless hours spent at the Academy library, but she hadn't received the pleasure of seeing one in real life. With magic to do everything for them, sorcerers had no use for cars or any other kind of mortal transportation.

"Sabrina, do you have any mortal cash on you? I have some, but not enough for three tickets," Sylvester said as he pulled out his wallet and eyed a sign on the bus stating how much tickets were.

"Um, yeah, I think I have some," Sabrina replied as she reached into her skirt pocket.

Aureum noticed Sabrina pausing with her hand in her pocket, almost dazed for a second, before getting back on track and pulling out some mortal money.

Mortal money was another thing that Aureum hadn't yet seen up close. It was all so intriguing and new.

"I hope this will cover it," Sabrina said as she handed the money to Sylvester.

Sorcerer money looked very different from mortal money.

They didn't have green paper with weird faces on them.

Instead, they had circular coins that were usually made out of various precious gems and materials like silver.

To top it off, they had triangular shapes punched into the center of circular coins with their ancient language, Bermuda, written around the coin's edges.

Sylvester eyed the money that Sabrina gave him and nodded. "Yes, it should be enough." The bus door opened up, and a mortal sat in the front; Aureum assumed it was the bus driver. The bus driver was a very oversized man in a blue uniform with donut stains on his shirt. The man suddenly honked the horn, causing the trio to jump from surprise.

"Hey, you kids getting on, or what? I don't have all day!" he yelled, clearly not in a good mood.

"Come on. Let's go." Sylvester took the lead and walked up into the bus. He whispered something to the bus driver that Sabrina and Aureum couldn't hear, handed him the wad of money, and made his way toward the back of the bus.

This made Aureum even more unsure of Sylvester.

The trio sat from the back.

Aureum and Sabrina shared a seat while Sylvester sat in the seat across from them.

Aureum sat against the window with Sabrina near the aisle.

Sylvester stared out the window as the bus started up. Besides the trio and the bus driver, there was only one other person on the bus with them. She wished that she knew where they were going, but Sylvester wouldn't tell her or Sabrina anything. It was as if Sylvester didn't trust them with information. Aureum sighed.

She had her backpack on her lap, and so did Sabrina.

Sabrina suddenly jumped when Chi chirped as he awoke from his nap.

"My gosh. I am not going to get used to seeing a chick with horns. Speaking of which, why didn't the bus driver freak out about the chicken?" Sabrina asked after she recomposes herself.

Aureum smiled and patted Chi on the head. "Mortals don't have the mental capacity to see or understand what we do," she began, feeling slightly like a history teacher as Sabrina listened intently. "The Mortal Realm has a thick layer of magic around it, concealing our oddities from mortals' eyes. If mortals caught a single glance at something from our realm, they'd go crazy."

"This is so confusing. So, what, you're telling me is that there is some sort of … blanket or barrier thing that keeps the magical stuff hidden?"

Aureum shrugged. "More or less. Every realm has its own version of it."

"Ugh," Sabrina grumbles.

"How about I tell you more about the Sorcerer Realm? To help you understand more," Aureum offered, feeling bad for Sabrina's confusion. "It might help to have some background information on it. You never know. I mean, you are a part of it, after all."

Sabrina nodded. "Sure, enlighten me," she said as she leaned back against the bus seat.

As Sabrina did so, Chi chirped again and hopped down from Aureum's shoulder and into Aureum's lap. She smiled at him. She loved her little companion.

Sabrina said, "For starters, how did that happen?" She gestured to Chi.

"What do you mean?" Aureum asked, genuinely confused.

"How did … How is that even possible? How can—um, what's the chicken's name?"

Aureum smiled. "His name is Chi."

"Right. Thanks. Um, anyway, how did he get horns? It's just so … unnatural."

Aureum frowned. "What do you mean?"

"Well, in the Mortal Realm, we have chickens, but they don't have horns," Sabrina replied. Realization dawned on Aureum's face before she burst into laughter. "What's so funny?" Sabrina asks, clearly flustered.

"I finally understood what you were asking me," Aureum said after she calmed down. "Chi isn't a normal chicken, like the ones you would find in your realm. Well, he was in the beginning, but when I was younger, I was messing around with some potions. I was trying a new formula when Chi came in and accidentally knocked over a bunch of potions on himself. Long story short, it gave him these horns and made him unable to grow any bigger than the size he is now. He can still function properly; he simply doesn't get any bigger than this."

"Oh," Sabrina replied, taking it all in. "Care to shed some light on more information about not just the Sorcerer Realm, but other realms in general?"

"Sure thing. The question is where to start …" Aureum hummed aloud in thought before snapping her fingers. "I've got it. How about I tell you about the parallel realms?"

Sabrina shrugged. "Yeah, have at it. I know nothing, so I'm all ears."

"Okay, great! This is one of my favorite things to talk and learn about. Basically, almost every known realm has a parallel. For example, the Sorcerer and the Mortal Realms are parallels. If one goes, so does the other. They anchor each other, but at the same time, they're total opposites."

"Is that a good thing or a bad thing?" Sabrina asked, looking confused already.

Aureum shrugged. "Eh … both? It really depends on the situation."

"Alright then," Sabrina responded slowly.

"Oh, how about I teach you how to read Bermuda? Like I told you in Alchemy, it was the original language spoken by many people of various realms. Of course, other languages were created, and Bermuda is now very rarely spoken in conversation, but a lot of the old text is still in Bermuda. Not to mention that the teachers like to quiz us on it here and there." Aureum unzipped her backpack.

"So it's like an almost dead language that's trying to still stay alive?" Sabrina suggested.

"I guess that's one way to put it." Aureum agreed as she pulled out an old library textbook from her backpack. Aureum adored books in general, but she especially loves old library books. The covers were so pretty and made them look so elegant. Just like the one she had in her hands. It had a beautiful purple cover with golden designs on it.

"You brought some old books along? What about your clothes and other essentials?" Sabrina blurted.

Aureum chuckled softly as her cheeks turned the faintest shade of pink. "I like to read, and I borrowed them from the Academy library the other day. I figured to grab them because they contained some old spells, incantations, chants, hexes, jinxes, and things like that. I thought maybe I could try to teach you more—if you're interested, of course."

Sabrina nodded slowly. Aureum grinned and excitedly began to teach Sabrina about the Sorcerer Realms, the other known realms, and countless spells.

"This spell can be used to bring someone back to life, but it's hardly ever used because the consequences could be disastrous. I recommend not using it unless the stakes are high and it's absolutely necessary," Aureum began, pointing to a bunch of symbols that Sabrina couldn't make sense of. "Now, this spell can be used for levitation." Aureum pressed her lips together and fished her hand around back in her backpack. She pulled out a pencil and placed it on the book. "I'll show you how to pronounce it."

Both girls weren't aware of how much time had gone by but Sabrina soon grew tired, and they decided to take a break.

Aureum eventually drifted off with her head leaning against the window while the bus continued on to their unknown destination.

Boom!

Aureum's eyes snapped open, and she immediately was on full alert. It happened so quickly that Aureum didn't have time to process it all. One second she was sleeping on the bus, and the next second she found herself on the pavement on the side of the road. Aureum could feel intense heat as she rolled over from her back and onto her stomach before pushing herself up to her feet. She glanced around for her backpack and found it lying a few feet away from her, covered in ashes.

Aureum quickly snatched it and put it on her back.

"Aureum!" she heard a distant voice yell.

Aureum's head was spinning, and all of her senses were thrown off. She turned her head and gasped as she saw the bus turned on its side with fire everywhere.

What the heck happened?

Did we get hit by another car?

There seemed to be no sign of danger, which made Aureum very anxious.

If there's no immediate sign of danger or threat, then how did the bus get turned over and on fire?

This is madness.

"Oh, my gosh," Aureum said with wide eyes. She clutched her belt in an attempt to calm herself down. Then an unnerving thought came to her.

Where is Chi?

What if Chi—no.

He didn't.

He's here and alive.

He has to be!

Aureum frantically searched for her little friend. Her heart was racing as she ran around, only to feel a sharp pain in her ankle. It caused her to lose her balance and fall down onto the pavement again. She grunted in pain.

Sabrina ran toward her and knelt down beside her. "What happened? Are you okay?" Sabrina blurted as she analyzed Aureum.

"I … I don't know what happened. I was just waking up from a nap, and then there was a loud explosion. Next thing I know, I'm on the ground with my foot in the wrong direction. I think I blacked out for a minute or so. Where's Sylvester and Chi? Have you seen them?" Aureum asked as Sabrina's attention moved to Aureum's foot.

"Yes and no," Sabrina replied, shaking her head in distress.

Aureum felt like crying. Continuous pain shot up from her ankle, but she knew that she had to keep it together.

"I haven't seen Sylvester, but I found Chi," Sabrina said as she pointed to the little chick sitting on her shoulder, looking unharmed and unaffected by the current events.

Aureum let out a sigh of relief as Sabrina gently picked up Chi and passed Chi to her. Chi chirped happily (or at least, Aureum thought it was happily) as she took him into her arms. "Oh, thank goodness you're okay, Chi! I'm so sorry about bringing you along. I should've left you at the Academy with Fern, where you would've been safer," Aureum murmured sadly as she pet Chi's head.

Chi chirped again, making Aureum wish that there was a spell that she could use to talk to him. "Thank you, Sabrina," Aureum said, looking at Sabrina with newfound respect and genuine gratitude. "What about you? Are you okay?" Aureum asked, feeling guilty for only thinking of her own pain and not of her friend.

Sabrina shrugged and held her left wrist with her right hand.

It looked slightly bent out of shape with multiple cuts across it.

"You're welcome, and I'm fine, I think. I just hurt my wrist, but it'll heal. It's just a little blood, not toxic waste. You, on the other hand, need medical attention." Sabrina helped up Aureum, allowing Aureum to lean onto her.

Aureum grunted and shook her head. "No, I'm okay. Just get me over to the sand. I know a healing spell to fix this," she replied. Sabrina helped her limp over to the side of the road. Sabrina gently lowered Aureum down so she could sit as comfortable as possible, not putting pressure into her foot. "Also, Sabrina, you're not fine. That's a lot of blood. You must've hit your wrist on something sharp and it cut it." Aureum studied Sabrina's wounded wrist.

Sabrina waved her hand in dismissal. "Like I said before, it's just a little blood. I'm okay. I'll live. Now, how about that healing spell?"

"Oh yeah. I almost forgot about it. Um, just hold out your wrist," she instructs, and Sabrina obliged.

Aureum closed her eyes and mumbled an old healing spell in Bermuda. As she did so, the open cuts on Sabrina's wrist began to heal. The skin morphed itself back together, and the blood on her wrist vanished.

When Aureum finished, she noticed Sabrina watching in amazement with wide eyes. "Wow! That's amazing!" Sabrina laughed, lightening the mood.

Aureum cracked a small smile and nodded. "Yep. It comes in handy every now and then. Now I'll heal my foot."

Sabrina kept quiet as Aureum repeated the spell and felt her ankle fixing itself.

Aureum let out a sigh of relief when she felt it magically mended. She got up to her feet, testing her foot, and Sabrina stayed right next to her, ready to catch her if she stumbled. "It's good as new. All better," Aureum confirmed

Sabrina smiled. "That's awesome!" she said again.

"Sabrina! Aureum!"

Aureum jumps at the sound of Sylvester's voice, and the girls turn to see a figure running toward them. As Sylvester got closer, Aureum could see him more clearly. His brown trench coat was covered in dirt, and his face had some scratches, but other than that he looked fine.

"Sylvester!" Sabrina called back, clearly relieved that he was alive and well.

"I'm so glad you both are okay," Sylvester said as he panted heavily and tried to catch his breath.

"Yeah, we're fine. We got a little banged up, but Aureum used a cool healing spell to fix us," Sabrina recalled, and Sylvester smiled.

Aureum suddenly frowned when she remembered the bus. "I still can't believe that the bus exploded, like that. How did it even happen?" she asked, earning Sylvester and Sabrina's attention. She looked over to the exploded bus, where police and fire trucks were currently tending to it, helping the bus driver and only remaining passenger out to safety.

Fortunately the trio was far enough away from the chaos that the police did not notice them. Sylvester shifted awkwardly on his feet. "Actually, about that …"

Aureum raised an eyebrow, and Sabrina crossed her arms as she looked at him.

"About what?" Sabrina said sharply.

"I may or may not have been the reason that the bus blew up," he mumbled shamefully.

"You what? Why? How?" Aureum exclaimed in sudden shock and anger.

"I'll explain later, when we find some place to stay tonight. Let's get you healed, and then we can find a motel or something to stay in for the night," Sylvester said as he fiddled with his wrist watch. Sabrina and Aureum frowned, not liking that he was avoiding Aureum's question.

Aureum sighed in frustration. Sylvester was on her last nerve.

First he ignores Sabrina and me, and then he refuses to answer my important questions.

Next, he claims to have been the reason why the bus blew up, but refuses give a reason as to why or how.

Aureum wondered how Sabrina was feeling about all of this, and the girls followed Sylvester in search of a place to stay for the night. She hoped he got over whatever he was going through soon.

For some odd reason, Sylvester seemed to know his way around wherever they were, and he led them to a run-down motel. Aureum wanted to ask him where exactly they were and if they were in Flordia yet, but she decided to keep her mouth shut because she figured that he wouldn't tell them anyway.

The trio entered the motel, and Aureum decided to focus on admiring the Mortal Realm and its strange creations instead of constantly questioning Sylvester's tactics.

They reached the front desk and were greeted by an older lady with a grim and dull expression on her face. Wrinkles covered her hands and face, and she glared at us when they walked over. Aureum's eyes scanned her name tag, which read, "Aggie."

"Can I help you?" Aggie grumbled in a tired, nasally voice.

"Um, yes, actually. We would like to book a room for one night," Sylvester answered with a polite smile.

Aggie sighed, unfazed by his politeness. "Okay. A room for how many?"

"Three," Sylvester responded, trying to stay polite despite the fatigue in his voice and the lady's rudeness.

"One night for three people will be five hundred dollars," Aggie muttered.

Sabrina's eyes widened. "Five hundred…? Sylvester, we don't have—"

Sylvester put a finger to his lips and glared at Sabrina, but Aureum couldn't help but agree. She didn't have any mortal money, and Sabrina used most of hers for the bus ride. Sabrina reluctantly snapped her mouth shut but let out a huff of annoyance, and Aureum frowned.

There was no way that Sylvester could sweet-talk his way out of this. This would be crazy.

But much to Aureum and Sabrina's surprise, Sylvester closed his eyes, exhaled deeply, and recomposed himself. He straightened his posture and then reopened his eyes. Sylvester stared into Aggie's eyes and firmly said, "You will let us stay the night for free."

Sabrina gawked in awe as Aggie's eyes glazed over and her head twitched. Aureum felt her body tense as it clicked in her mind regarding what Sylvester was doing. He was using a very old—and a very much forbidden—spell that could be used to manipulate non-sorcerers. It took magic from the Dark Realm, and if one didn't use it correctly, it could take over and kill the one using it, if he was not strong enough to control it.

And if the person was strong enough, it could still mess with the user's mind and create a not-so-good situation. Aureum was tempted to tell Sylvester to stop, but she couldn't bring herself to. The women's mouth stayed firmly shut as if refusing to say anything back, and Aureum felt slightly relieved. It wasn't working.

But much to her dismay, Sylvester wasn't ready to give up. Sylvester let out a huff of annoyance and sternly repeated himself. "You *will* let us stay the night for free."

Aggie's eyes remained glazed over with a dazed look in them as she finally replied with, "You know what? Five hundred dollars? That's ridiculous! Don't worry about it. Let me lead you to your room for the night." Aggie smiled brightly, but Aureum knew that it was fake. It made her feel sick to her stomach.

"Sylvester, what did you just do? What Star Wars voodoo trick did you just use?" Sabrina demanded to know in a hushed yet threatening voice, clearly horrified and confused as to what had just happened.

Sylvester elbowed Sabrina in the side and shushed her as the trio followed Aggie around the corner to their temporary dorm. They walked down a somewhat long hallway and stopped at a room with the number 523 written in silver on it.

"Here are your keys. There's a swimming pool out front with a hot tub. Enjoy your stay." Aggie beamed, still under the dark spell as she then turned around and walked like a zombie back to her desk.

Aureum let out a breath that she hadn't known she had been holding. "How could you do that, Sylvester? To that poor old lady!" she screeched, clearly outraged with Sylvester's behavior. It caused Sabrina to flinch. Aureum wasn't one to lose her cool, but this really got under her skin.

She couldn't keep it in as Sylvester unlocked the door and walked inside with the two girls trailing behind him. She had her hands on her hips with a furious expression on her face.

"I don't know what you're talking about, Aureum. All I know is that I got us a room to stay the night for free." He shrugged carelessly as he took off his backpack. He tossed it onto the couch that was pushed up against the back wall, opposite of two twin-sized beds in the one-roomed apartment.

Aureum let out a huff of annoyance and retorted, "You used dark magic, Sylvester! That's forbidden! When you start using dark magic to get people to do your dirty deeds, that's when you start to change!" She took off her own backpack and placed it down on one of the beds.

Sabrina stood there awkwardly, not understanding what was happening as usual. "I'm not going to change, Aureum. We needed a place to stay, just for one night. Using the hypnotizing spell for one tiny little favor won't kill anybody!" Sylvester retorted as he took off of his trench coat and slung it over his chair.

Sabrina exhaled deeply in frustration before yelling, "Hey!" This caused both Sylvester and Aureum to stop arguing and turn to look at her. "I don't know what the heck is going on around here, but as of now I don't care. I'm going for a walk, and I'm taking the room keys with me." Sabrina snatched the keys off of the TV stand where Sylvester had placed them.

"Sabrina," Sylvester began, but Sabrina held up a hand to cut him off.

"No. Just don't. I need to think. I'll be back soon." Sabrina then took her backpack off and left it by one of the twin beds before storming out of the room, leaving Sylvester and Aureum alone.

VIII. "Warriors in Pajamas"

Sabrina needed some space and some fresh air.

She hated it when people fought; it really got under her skin.

Aureum and Sylvester weren't even trying to reason with each other, which also led to Sabrina's fit of anger. She knew that if she was going to get better, she needed to step outside and temporarily get away from the stress. It wasn't just their fighting that had set her off. She felt like she was under so much pressure and her mind was going a hundred miles per hour, trying to wrap her head around every new thing that she learned.

It wasn't going too well.

Sabrina exhaled deeply as she walked aimlessly down hallways, not caring where she was going as long as she could be by herself and cool off.

Did she feel guilty for just blowing up on Sylvester and Aureum like that?

Yes and no.

They both weren't accomplishing anything, so when Sabrina yelled at them, it broke up the fight. Now that she'd left then alone, they could figure out whatever their issue was.

Sabrina continued to walk down a long hallway, and the end drew near. She recognized that she had only walked back to where they had first come in. Coming into view was the front desk.

Sabrina expected to see Aggie there, back to her normal self, but oddly enough, no one was there.

The hotel seemed to be abandoned, with no one there except Sabrina and her friends. Sabrina noticed that the main lights were off; the only light was the small glow of light that seeped out from underneath other doors.

Sighing, Sabrina was about to turn back to the room when she spotted a map on Aggie's desk. She chewed on the inside of her cheek in thought, tempted to take it in order to look at where they were. Sabrina didn't like taking things without permission, but she was possibly on a suicide mission with a guide who wouldn't tell her or Aureum anything.

Sabrina believed that she and Aureum deserved to know where they were and what was happening.

Mustering up some courage and pushing the guilt aside, Sabrina reached her hand across the desk and snatched the map.

It's only a map, Sabrina told herself, trying to make the guilt that kept building up go away. She then let out a deep breath and turned the map around so that she could read it.

"Miami, Florida," the top of it read.

Sabrina gave a sigh of relief. That was where Sylvester had wanted them to be, because it was the closest opening to the Bermuda Triangle, which is where they would find Caspian and Sabrina could rescue her Dad. Sabrina felt a lot better about the whole situation as she put the map back.

Sabrina suddenly jumped as she heard the sound of a women's voice behind her. She whipped around to see that a small TV that was hung in the corner of the room had turned on.

"I am Jane Winters, reporting live at an interstate just off of the outskirts of Miami, Florida, where a recent bus explosion has occurred. You heard it right, folks—a bus explosion. As far as we know, no one on the bus was injured. There were four passengers on the bus and the driver. Only one passenger was found, and the other three have vanished from the scene. Could the three passengers who fled the scene be terrorists in disguise? Escapees from prison, perhaps? As of now, those questions are left unanswered, but we have police on the case …"

Sabrina stopped listening after that and dashed back down the hallway to her room.

Great, now I'm a fugitive.

She rolled her eyes at the thought.

This is exactly what I needed.

Perfect.

Sabrina sighed in frustration as she fished the room keys out of her pocket, her hand touching her phone. She hadn't used it since she had left for the Sorcerer's Realm with Sylvester.

After a little mental debate, Sabrina took her phone out of her pocket and pressed her lips together into a thin line, in thought.

She noticed that the screen was slightly cracked from the bus explosion. She pressed the power button, and much to her relief, it turned on.

The battery percentage was really low, almost to red, but there was cell service.

Sabrina thought that she could call Aunt Jeanette to assure her that she was okay and that she'd hopefully be home soon.

Sabrina swallowed hard and swiped her phone to where she could call someone. Sabrina pushed her home phone number, praying that someone would answer. She leaned against the wall, feeling a wave of anxiety crash over her. She didn't know what she would say or how Aunt Jeanette would react—or if she'd even pick up.

"Hello?" a quiet voice said from the other line.

"*Paris?*" Sabrina said in surprise.

"Sabrina? What? But you … how are you?" Paris began to ramble.

Sabrina cut her off. "Paris, my phone doesn't have much battery left, so please listen. I want you and Aunt Jeanette to know that I'm …" Sabrina glanced at the door where Sylvester and Aureum were and let out a small sigh. "I'm safe, and I'll be home soon. I hate making promises, but this is one that I'll make and keep. I'm on an important mission right now, so please don't try to call back. I don't have my phone charger, and my phone is probably going to die soon. Please tell Demi and Jason that I'm not, you know, dead. And—oh, shoot." Sabrina looked at her phone and realized it had 3 percent battery left. "Paris, remember that I love you. You and Aunt Jeanette are the only family that I've ever known, and I don't know what I'd do without you. I'll be home soon, and—" Before Sabrina could continue, the conversation was cut short because her phone had run out of battery.

Sabrina sighed, feeling a little annoyed that she couldn't say more, but what was done was done. She stuffed her phone back into her skirt pocket, let out a breath to compose herself, and opened the door to the room in which she would be spending the night.

She found Sylvester lying on the couch and staring blankly up at the wall, his eyebrows furrowed and an unreadable expression plastered on his face. He was resting his head on his hands and seemed deep in thought.

Meanwhile, Aureum was sitting on her bed, reading one of the spell books that she had showed Sabrina on the bus quietly to herself.

Even though the silence was slightly unnerving, Sabrina was grateful for the fact that they weren't fighting.

"So did you guys make up?" Sabrina asked, hope evident in her voice.

Sylvester glanced over at her from his spot on the couch and shrugged. Aureum glanced up from her book, looked over at Sylvester and then Sabrina, and shook her head in defeat. "I don't know. I still don't agree with what he did. It's dark magic, and it scares me. But I suppose that if he doesn't do it again unless absolutely necessary, then we're good."

Sabrina looked at Sylvester with her arms crossed and an eyebrow raised. "Well?"

"Well, what?" Sylvester replied with a strange calmness in his voice.

"Can you two please make up? If we're going to defeat this Caspian guy, then we all need to be on the same page. We all need to trust each other," Sabrina said as she made her way over to what she assumed was her bed and unzipped her backpack.

As Sabrina took out a pair of pajamas, Sylvester let out a sigh and grumbled, "All right, fine! I won't do dark magic again unless it's a life-or-death situation. Are we good?" He looked over at Aureum with a raised eyebrow.

Aureum smiled and gives a small nod of approval. "Okay, we're good."

"Great! I'm happy you guys made up. Now, I'm going to go shower because of obvious reasons." Sabrina gestured to her appearance. Mud, blood, sweat and dirt covered her, and besides all of that, Sabrina simply needed a shower to wash all of her worries away, even if it was only temporarily. She left the room and headed toward the bathroom, which wasn't too terrible considering that they staying in a pretty run-down motel.

Although it did have that eerie feeling to it and didn't smell the best, it wasn't the worst bathroom that Sabrina had been in.

When Sabrina got out of the shower, Aureum quickly jumped up to race in after her.

Meanwhile, Sylvester took the room keys and excused himself, saying that he needed a breath of fresh air. He looked a little pale and shaken up, but Sabrina was sure that it was nothing too serious.

She then brushed out the knots in her hair before snuggling into bed underneath the not-so-warm and thin motel bedsheets, attempting to fall asleep.

Sabrina didn't manage to fall asleep that night.

Aureum had come out of the shower, and Sabrina had pretended to be asleep. Aureum soon fell asleep herself, and Sabrina was left alone in the dark, with only the sound of Sylvester's soft snoring and Aureum's quiet breathing.

Sabrina didn't know why she wasn't tired. The day had been insanely long and crazy, and there was no reason why Sabrina shouldn't be tired.

But for some odd reason, no matter what Sabrina did, she couldn't manage to fall asleep.

She tried counting sheep, but no matter how high she counted, she couldn't fall asleep. All she could focus on was the snoring, light breathing, passing cars, and the sound of something tapping on the window.

Sabrina had the strangest feeling that something was watching her, that she wasn't the only one awake in the room. It made her stomach churn, and she tried to keep herself calm.

Sabrina tried telling herself that it was nothing to worry about and that she was just being paranoid. It didn't work.

So there Sabrina lay, too scared to sleep, with pitch darkness for her vision.

Sabrina readjusted her position in her bed, moving from her side onto her back. The bed wasn't the most comfortable thing to sleep on, but Sabrina had slept on worst. She exhaled deeply and covered her face with her hands.

"Why can't I just fall asleep?" Sabrina grumbled quietly with her eyes tightly closed.

Then she suddenly heard the sound of the floor creaking. Her eyes snapped open, and she removed her hands from her face. She held her breath when she saw the shadow of a man standing before her.

It was a tall man, his figure like a shadow with pure white sunken eyes.

The shadowed man and Sabrina seemed to be having a staring contest—until he let out an inhuman hiss and lunged toward her bed.

Sabrina let out a scream and heard Sylvester yell, "Sabrina, get out of the way!"

Sabrina tossed her bed covers aside and leaped out of her bed, rolling off the edge and landing stomach first on the floor. Sabrina's heart raced as Aureum got out of bed as well, tiredly trying to figure out what was happening. Then Aureum's eyes widened, and she yelled, "Oh, my gosh! It's a Nightshade!"

Sabrina's breathing became rapid, in short and quick breaths recalling what the creature was capable of and what she had learned about it before they left for their quest. If she could remember correctly, they were Caspian's minions. They were made of dark magic and were able to morph into whatever they pleased and posses someone if they desired. Then they could kill what they possessed if they wanted and use the new body at free will.

Fun.

Sylvester casted a spell and blasted a beam of golden light at the shadow man. The shadow man turned around to fight back, only to be struck dead in the chest and dispersed into dust.

"Oh, my god," Sabrina gasped in horror.

"Come on. Get up," Sylvester said as he went to Sabrina and pulled her up to her feet.

Sabrina was shaking so badly that she thought her knees would collapse.

Aureum was awake and alert, with her bag slung over her shoulder and a determined yet terrified expression on her face. "We need to get out of here before more of those things come!" she exclaimed frantically, fear written all over her face. Chi sat on her shoulder, not showing any sign of fear—but then again, he was just a chicken and probably had no idea as to what was going on.

"Grab what you need from your bags, and leave what you can live without behind. Put on your cloaks, and let's go." Sylvester's strictness was evident in his voice as he shoved his trench coat over his pajamas and then put on his cloak.

Aureum and Sabrina nodded and put on their cloaks.

Sabrina's cloak was shaking for some reason, but Sabrina did her best to ignore it. It was so strange. It was as if the cloak had a mind of its own and was reacting to what was happening around them.

But Sabrina didn't have the time to ponder the thought now.

Sabrina knitted her eyebrows together as she took what she needed from her backpack and stuffed it into her pajama pockets.

Thank goodness she had pockets.

Sabrina had taken her phone and some leftover money that she had. Fortunately, when Sabrina had packed, she'd left anything that was really important back at the Academy, not knowing what the future would hold for her.

Sabrina noticed that Aureum was clutching two spell books to her chest (which Sabrina recognized to be the two books that they had been looking at together on the bus) as they walked down the hallway. Sabrina followed Sylvester and Aureum, her mind trying to piece together what was happening.

"This is bad. This is really, really bad. Because that one Nightshade found us, Caspian now knows where we are, or at least he has an idea since that Nightshade almost killed you. I'm sure that more are on their way. He will send an army of them now that he knows that we're here." Sylvester rambled as the trio approached the front desk.

"But if Caspian has been making enough of those Nightshades to create an army, then how come none of them have attack me before? I've never seen them around or anything," Sabrina said feeling lost.

"Caspian must not have manipulated them enough, or made the right formula for them to be able to track you down. If he did, you'd be dead, and he'd have all control." Sylvester responded as he fished his hand around in his pocket for something.

Sylvester pulls out a ten-dollar bill from his pocket and put it on the counter. "I know that it's not much, but at least it's something," he muttered. "Now, Aureum, do you really need those spell books? They'll get heavy and become a pain to carry. Just leave them here."

Aureum's face turned to horror.

"Leave them here? But they're library books! I can't just leave them! Do you know how much trouble I could get into?" she squeaked.

Sylvester exhales in frustration. "Then stuff them in your belt pockets or something. I don't know, but right now we have more important matters at hand than spell books."

"But what if a mortal finds them? We have to take them with us!" she insisted.

Sylvester gritted his teeth in annoyance, but Sabrina could tell that he was giving in. "Fine! Give them to me, and I'll put them in my hidden trench coat pockets."

Aureum nodded and passed him the two spell books.

Sabrina quietly watched as Sylvester tucked them safely inside his two giant pockets.

Sylvester moved quickly as the trio headed out of the motel. "If that one Nightshade found us, then more must be on the way. It probably smelt Sabrina's presence or something like that."

"It can smell me? Do I really smell *that* bad?" Sabrina asked, slightly offended as they reached the exit of the motel.

Sylvester laughed dryly as they step outside into the dark, cold, midnight air, getting drenched in the evening rain. "It's not necessarily your actual smell but your unique blood. No one else in the world—that we know of—has the blood of both a mortal and a sorcerer. Your blood is different, unique, special—and deadly. But enough about that. We need to keep moving."

Sylvester suddenly froze in his tracks as the trio entered the motel parking lot. Sabrina frowned. "Sylvester, what's wrong?"

"Oh, my god," Aureum breathed in bewilderment.

Sabrina pushed her way past the two so that she could see.

The trio was already surrounded.

More of those Nightshades had found them already, as Sylvester had predicted.

"We're completely surrounded! What's our exit strategy?" Aureum asked frantically.

Sylvester raised an eyebrow. *"Exit strategy?"*

Sabrina felt herself becoming pale. "Oh, my god, we're all going to die!"

"N-no worries! We're completely surrounded, so that means we can, um, attack in any direction!" Sylvester grinned, attempting to lighten the mood but failing miserably.

The three of them were surrounded by about three dozen nightshades, some taking on the form of a human while others morphed into various creatures.

The Nightshades began snarling and creeping in on them. Sabrina held her breath, fearing that this was the end.

"Hey, you guys. Remember when I blew up that bus?" Sylvester asked as the three of them stood back to back, ready to fight.

"Um, kind of hard to forget. It was only, what, a few hours ago?" Sabrina deadpanned.

Sylvester let out a huff of annoyance but then said, "Yeah, I didn't just blow it up to blow it up. One of the Nightshades found us there, and I thought by killing it off, more wouldn't come. My spell went wrong, and the entire bus ended up exploding. The nightshade got away. It must've followed us to the motel and called the rest of its friends to ambush us."

Sabrina groaned again. "You're kidding me, right?"

Sylvester laughed awkwardly. "Oh, how I wish I was!"

"If this is the end, I just want you guys to know that you're the coolest friends I've ever had! And Sabrina, next time you ask me to sneak out with you on a quest, my answer will be no!" Aureum exclaimed.

"I love you too, Aureum!" Sabrina called back sarcastically.

That was when everything was went spiraling downhill.

The next few minutes happened in a blur.

The creatures pounced on them in practically perfect unison, as if it had been rehearsed. Sabrina remembered trying to cast spells to hold them back, but only a couple spells succeeded.

Then something hit her in the back of her head, and the last thing she remembered before blacking out was Aureum's cry of horror.

The second that Sabrina regained consciousness, she immediately wished that she hadn't.

At first, she thought that she was dead.

But after pain struck her hard with no mercy, it gave her a clear wake-up call that she was still very much alive.

Sabrina didn't know what had hit her in the back of her head, but she was determined to get her revenge on whatever it was.

Sabrina's eyelids felt heavy, and she had a pounding headache.

Slowly and tiredly, Sabrina peeled open her eyes, her vision slightly blurry and taking to adjust.

"Sabrina? Oh, my gosh, you're okay!" Sabrina heard Aureum cry with relief. Sabrina gave a groan in response. She was too tired to speak, and all she wanted to do was fall back asleep. "Here, let me help you sit up."

Sabrina kept her eyes closed as she focused on the sounds around her. She could make out Aureum walking toward her, and then Aureum carefully helped her up into a sitting position.

Sabrina hated that she felt so weak.

"Wh ... what happened?" Sabrina attempted to say as she finally managed to open her eyes, but it came out more as gibberish.

"Careful, Sabrina. You got hit pretty hard in the head. Also, I have no idea as to what you just said," Aureum said.

Sabrina groaned again and placed her head in her hands.

She noticed the floor that she was sitting on was solid and concrete. Her vision slowly came into better focus.

Even more disturbing, Sabrina realized that they were in a room that very much resembled a jail cell.

"Mr. Banner?" Aureum asked, confusing Sabrina slightly. "Sabrina's awake."

"Sabrina? Oh, thank goodness!" A deeper voice replied with joy. Sabrina heard footsteps quickly rush toward her, and a pair of strong arms wrapped her into a hug. "You scared me so badly, Sabrina. Don't you ever do that again!" the man chided.

"I'm sorry, but should I know you?" Sabrina managed to get out. She pulled herself out of the man's embrace and scooted away enough so she could see his appearance.

"No, you shouldn't. You were only a small child. I never got to meet you. I had no idea that Aurora was pregnant with you until it was too late. I was on my way to the Mortal Realm a few years after Caspian had attacked the Academy, as I'm sure you've learned about," the man said, and Sabrina nodded.

"When I got here, I went back to the place where I had learned was Aurora's home, but I hadn't known that she had been dead for three years that another family had moved in. I figured that she had moved away or something. When I went to turn back to the Sorcerer Realm that was when

Caspian's nightshades jumped me. They took me as prisoner and brought me here. To be trapped in the Bermuda Triangle along with Caspian."

"Wait, where in the Bermuda Triangle are we exactly, anyway?" Aureum asked, as if reading Sabrina's thoughts.

"I'm not entirely sure. I've been trapped here for twelve years now, give it take. All I know is that we're in some sort of cave on a beach near the edge of the Bermuda Triangle," the man replied.

Aureum nodded in acknowledgment, taking in the somewhat helpful information. Sabrina took in the man's appearance.

He had long, messy, windswept, dirty blonde hair with locks that had turned silver from age along with an unshaven chin.

He had wrinkles under his eyes, on his cheeks, and on his hands, presumably from old age.

"How do I know that you're actually who you claim to be?" Sabrina asked, not wanting to trust this strange man too soon.

"You have every right to not trust me, Sabrina. But tell me everything that you've learned since you've learned about the Sorcerer Realm."

"Why ...?" Sabrina began, but the man cut her off.

"I just want to know how much you've learned. I would hate it if Sylvester blindly dragged you into this mess," he replied earnestly.

Sabrina sighed. "All right. Well, I learned about my past, and about Caspian. I learned from Sylvester the other night that he knew where you were, and that Caspian had you held captive. But up until now, I didn't know why he wanted me or why I was involved in any of this. I know about my two souls, the prophecy, Angelica, the battle, the never-ending realms, and Caspian's Nightshades. Thanks to Aureum, I can read a little Bermuda as well as cast a couple spells."

The man let out a sigh of relief. "This is good. I'm grateful that you at least have an idea as to what's going on. I'll fill you in on the rest, and hopefully it'll convince you that I am who I claim to be."

Sabrina nodded, waiting for the man to continue.

The three of them were sitting in a circle.

The man's was leaning against the wall with a shackle latched around one of his ankles, forbidding him from going anywhere.

Aureum sat quietly, not asking questions and taking everything in.

Unlike Sabrina, who was loaded with questions and a desire to learn everything.

"Since you've learned of the battle and Caspian's nightshades along with all of that other jazz, I'm assuming that Sylvester told you of our first quest? Along with the multiple trips afterward that I made to visit your mother?"

The man who claimed himself to be Sabrina's father asked.

He closed his eyes as if to help himself remember.

"But only Sylvester knew about my last trip to the Mortal Realm, to visit Aurora after the battle with Caspian. I was fully aware of Aurora's pregnancy with you at the time, and I knew that I needed to visit her. I felt beyond guilty that your fate was already planned out by an old prophecy. I didn't tell anyone but Sylvester and your mother about your fate. That woman never left my mind. I couldn't bring myself to stay away. I found myself often daydreaming about her and wishing to be something more. I wished that either I lived there or she lived here, so that our love wouldn't be forbidden. There was something about that woman that I just couldn't let go. I loved Aurora very much, even though we never got to spend a lot of time together."

Frederick let out a sad sigh.

"I suppose by now, everyone's found out about my forbidden journey, but it's currently the least of my worries. When I made my final trip to the Mortal Realm, I had already been informed by Aurora that she had given birth to you. You were just a little baby at the time, when I first saw you."

Frederick opened his eyes to look over at Sabrina, who was listening to every word. "Up until now, that was the last time I saw you. I couldn't shake the guilt that you and your mother were in danger because of me. That has never left me. Your mother was fortunately a very wise women, and I trusted her with information about the Sorcerer Realm. That's how she knew that she needed to keep you safe. Aurora knew what I was, and she was fully aware of the realms. I knew that Aurora had to know, if we were to ever be together. I loved both you and your mother, Sabrina. Even though I didn't get to spend much time with you, I loved you very much, and I still do now. I hate Caspian for taking you away from me for so many years, even if you are forbidden." The man looked at Sabrina adoringly.

Sabrina shifted uncomfortably in her seat, not knowing how to respond.

How could she express her love to a man that she'd never met?

Frederick seemed to understand Sabrina's awkwardness and continued on with his story, not pressing her for a response.

Sabrina was grateful for it.

"I knew that I couldn't stay forever, especially because of who you now were. It became very clear to me that you were the prophecy child, and if I stayed around you, I was putting both you and your mother in harm's way. I went to leave, but that was when Caspian took me prisoner. One of his Nightshades tracked me here—I'm not sure how, but it did. Thankfully, I was nowhere near you and your mother, and so Caspian still didn't know where to find you. I've been Caspian's prisoner for a many long years. He's been pestering me and trying to get me to tell him of your location, but I refused. I wasn't going to give you up that easily."

Sabrina smiled faintly in gratitude.

"I learned that he was after you, not only because you were the prophecy child, but apparently because the curse that Angelica put on him. The curse could only be undone if a certain incantation was created with certain ingredients. A child born of both a mortal's and sorcerer's soul was required for the incantation, and I had just given him what he needed. Caspian began doing whatever he could to get any kind of Information out of me to find your location. He created more Nightshades, creatures made of dark magic with morphing and possessing abilities. But he made these ones differently. He used *my* blood in them, in the hopes of them now being able to sniff out your unusual blood. That's why Caspian's needs your two souls, and that's why you're the prophecy child. You're the last ingredient that he needs to break the curse and begin the rest of his plan to have ultimate control over all of the realms and live for eternity."

Frederick let out a sigh upon finishing his story.

Sabrina remained quiet for a moment, taking it all in.

She hoped that she wasn't going to regret her decision. "I believe you. I believe that you're my dad. It's going to take a lot to get used to saying that, though."

The man whom Sabrina would now call Dad smiled and embraced her tightly. "That's understandable, and thank you for believing me," he murmured as he hugged her. Sabrina forced a smile and hugged him back, still feeling uneasy about all of this. It was so much to take in, and it made her head spin.

"I see that you've gained Sabrina's trust, Freddie." An all-too-familiar voice suddenly said, making Sabrina's head perk up.

Sabrina pulled back from the hug and turned around to face the steel bars that kept the trio trapped in the prison cell. Sabrina gasped when she saw Sylvester walking toward them. She got up to her feet and ran towards the cell bars, grasping them tightly and pressing her face against them.

"You—you're here to help us! Right? And ... and you'll explain everything. You'll tell Aureum and me what happened and how we got here. You'll set us free, and we'll go stop Caspian—" She stopped midsentence when Sylvester held up a hand.

"I'm sorry, Sabrina, but I won't be doing any of that," Sylvester replied bluntly, no sympathy in his voice at all whatsoever.

Sabrina felt her shoulders drop, and she furrowed her eyebrows in puzzlement. "Wha—what do you mean? Of course you—no, you wouldn't ..." She shook her head, not wanting it to be true.

"Sylvester, you're alive!" Frederick exclaimed, shakily standing up and walking as close to the bars as the chain around his ankle would let him.

"Yes, I'm alive. But that doesn't matter right now. You all have visitor," Sylvester coldly replied as he stepped aside.

A tall man slowly walked in, taking his time with his hands held behind his back.

As the man walked closer, Sabrina studied his appearance.

The man walked with confidence, and a victorious smirk was on his lips. Sabrina assumed this was the infamous Caspian Mare, except more than ten years older than the painting that Sabrina had seen.

Caspian still had his black hair, but it was shaggier and messier, probably due to years of being trapped in the Mortal Realm with little access to magic. His eyes were still a dark black color with one eye being blind and bearing the scar.

Caspian still wore that black uniform from the painting, except now the uniform has various tears, dirt, and grime on it. His posture was no longer perfect, but slouched, and he was still very intimidating.

Not that Sabrina would admit that out loud, and especially not right in front of him.

Sabrina suddenly knew that the man in front of her was in fact Caspian Mare, and for once she didn't doubt herself.

The man smiled in a way that made Sabrina's blood run cold, and shivers went down her spine. She had no clue as to what his man was capable of, but if he had killed the headmistress before Amaris and had kept her dad as a prisoner for years, then he must be very powerful.

Caspian had a crazed look in his eyes as he studied Sabrina, his unnerving smirk never leaving his face.

"Well, isn't this nice," Caspian began, his voice slightly raspy with insanity evident in it. "What a lovely reunion, wouldn't you say? I'm glad that I finally got to meet you, Miss Sabrina. You're going to be the guest of honor this evening and a major part in my master plan. It can't be fulfilled without you, my dear. Thanks to Mr. Coulson, it now can be."

Caspian laughed but no one joined in, not even Sylvester. Caspian quickly composed himself and smirked. "I am Caspian Mare, as you may already know, and I will be your doom." He cackled.

Sabrina gulped. "Do I have a say in this?" she squeaked, mentally cursing herself for sounding so vulnerable and terrified.

"Nope!" He laughed like a madman, and Sabrina hated how carefree he was about all of this. "I told you I'd get your daughter in my possession, Frederick. You couldn't keep her location safe forever. Soon I will have eternal life and the ability to rip open portals to all of the realms. I will take total control from the Mortal to the Sorcerer, Dark, Astro, Monster, and countless other realms! Won't this be a treat?" Caspian giggled again like a spoiled kid on Christmas.

Sabrina swallowed hardly, mustering up some courage as she glared at him.

"Of course, you my dear Sabrina will be the guest of honor. Sadly, you won't be alive to witness my glory. But no matter! I'll remember to thank you. Now, we mustn't put this on hold any longer. Nice pajamas by the way, you two," Caspian said with a laugh, looking at Sabrina and Aureum.

The girls both glared at him and Sabrina ignored her slight embarrassment. "Let the elimination begin."

IX. "The Sword of a Half-Blood"

Sabrina's heart hammered rapidly against her chest.

Caspian continued to smirk, and a look of craziness flashed across his face as he commanded Sylvester to unlock the cell door.

Sylvester appeared to hesitate slightly before obliging Caspian's command.

He fished out a pair of keys from his pocket.

He puts the key into the keyhole on the cell door, which made Sabrina raise an eyebrow in surprise. Sabrina has expected the cell to be enchanted with magic or something like that, but it was a normal cage.

Sabrina's dad pushes himself up to his feet and stood in a stance that looked ready to pounce on Caspian. His face was full of anger and hatred. Sabrina had never seen so much loathing on one man's face.

"Back down, Frederick. You're only stalling your daughter's death. It will simply make it hurt more when she's dead," Caspian casually remarked with a yawn and a look of carelessness.

Sabrina's dad glared at Caspian.

"I've been your prisoner for thirteen aching years, Caspian. *Thirteen years* that I had to spend away from my daughter. *Thirteen years* of her childhood that I missed. Now that she's with me, I will not let her go again, no matter what you say or do," he snarled.

Sylvester looked startled by Frederick's determination and lack of fear.

Meanwhile, Caspian seemed bored and unfazed, although his lips twitched towards in amusement. "You make me laugh, Frederick. I do not fear you. I never have and never will. But you do fear me. I suggest you back down before things get ugly."

"Try me, Caspian," Frederick challenged as he puffed out his chest and stood with pride, trying to look threatening and fearless.

"Fine, but remember that you asked for it," Caspian warned, and his eyes landed on Sabrina. Caspian's eyes held a psychotic gleam and a lust for power.

"Now, rise, Sabrina Banner, and prepare for death," Caspian hissed, causing Sabrina to freeze up in fear.

She didn't know how to fight.

Heck, she barely knew how to cast a spell!

Not to mention that she was still in her pajamas, which was rather embarrassing.

She would be the laughingstock of the Sorcerer Realm for sure.

Sabrina exhaled deeply, mustering up some courage and swallowing her fear. She rose to her feet and gently pushed aside her dad.

"It's okay, Dad. I can fight my own battle," she whispered to him reassuringly.

He didn't seem the slightest bit convinced. "I know you can, and I trust you. But I just got you back. I can't lose you again," he murmured, a look of helplessness evident in his eyes. He seemed to be pleading for her to back down, but Sabrina's stubbornness and pride wouldn't let her.

Aureum was a few feet behind Sabrina's Dad, looking ready to fight if needed.

Sabrina was grateful that she had put her cloak on before they'd left the motel. Even if she didn't know many spells, at least she had a way to protect herself.

If Sabrina were to ever need the cloak, now was the time. Sabrina hoped that it would cooperate with her, which wasn't very often. The cloak seemed to have a mind of its own, and Sabrina was not very fond of it.

"Aw, how cute. A daddy-daughter moment. Too bad that there won't be time for any more of those!" Caspian laughed, taking Sabrina out of her thoughts. Sabrina glared at him in anger. "All right, let's get this over with. I have a whole bunch of realms to conquer." Caspian lazily rose his hand, and a ball of blue fire formed in it, making Sabrina gulp in slight terror.

Caspian's eyes lock with Sabrina, and she could feel her heart pounding against her chest as adrenaline coursed through her body, making her hands become slightly sweaty. She refuses to back down, despite every nerve in her body telling her to run.

I can do this.

Maybe I can't be stronger than him, but I can outsmart him.

Yeah, that's what I do.

I outsmart people.

I was never one for strength, but my intelligence always pulled through.

Sabrina's plan formed in her head.

Caspian shot the blue flames of magic from his hands.

Sabrina thought that Caspian was aiming for her, but his shot missed.

Sabrina felt so many mixed emotions within a fraction of a second. She was confused as to why Caspian had missed when he had a clear shot at her.

Maybe he was just one of those people with bad aim.

"Sabrina!" Sabrina heard her dad cry out. She whipped around and gasped in shock. She found Aureum and her dad standing like statues, frozen with the blue flames that had been around Caspian's hands now around them, like an aura, trapping them in place. Aureum looked furious yet terrified at the same time.

Aureum's face was scrunched up in frustration, and Sabrina could tell she was desperately trying to break free of the magic bond.

"How do I unfreeze you, or un-magic you, or whatever you call this?" Sabrina exclaimed frantically, her eyes wide in horror.

"Easy—you don't!" Caspian yelled from behind Sabrina.

Sabrina quickly spun back around and ducked just in time for Caspian to fire another blast of magic at her. She was breathing heavily and felt tired, even though the battle was just beginning. Sabrina would probably never live down the fact that after this is all over—if she survived—she battled a lunatic in her pajamas while wearing a lame superhero cape.

Oh, so heroic.

"Sabrina, use the spells I taught you on the bus!" Aureum cried out.

Sabrina felt all of the color drain from her face. "But I don't remember any of them! I don't even understand Bermuda!" she screamed back, wanting to break down and cry. Sabrina felt bad for screaming, but she was having a panic attack.

"Then don't use your magic! Just outsmart him!" Fred encouraged her.

Outsmart him.

Yeah.

I can do that.

Caspian laughed menacingly. She kept her eyes on him. "Just give up, Sabrina. This will all go a lot faster for you if you lay down your life right here, right now. I might even spare the ones you care most about when I rule, if you sacrifice yourself to me."

Sabrina wasn't having it. "Yeah, right!" she shot back. "Like I'd trust you to keep your word, you sick psycho!"

Caspian was fuming. "You *will* obey me, you annoying little girl! I will have your soul, and I will rule all!" He screamed like a two-year-old throwing a temper tantrum.

Outsmart him.

Outsmart him.

Outsmart him.

Come on, Sabrina!

Make him mad!

"You know, that's what every villain says before his plan ultimately fails!" Sabrina retorted with a smirk, faking confidence. Then a thought struck her.

Where did Sylvester go?

Sabrina didn't see the traitor anywhere, but she decided that it didn't matter right now. What mattered was keeping her head in the game and defeating Caspian.

"You're just a dumb little girl, who thinks she can actually survive this, *but you're wrong!*" Caspian screeched as he shot more colorful balls of flaming magic toward her.

Sabrina manages to dodge them, her cloak fortunately working with her and using its reflexes to help her maneuver around the magic balls.

Sabrina needed to take this fight out of this cell, away from her dad and Aureum. She didn't know whether magic could harm them while they were stunned like that, but she wasn't going to risk it. However, Sabrina was trapped.

Caspian was blocking her only exit, and it didn't look like he was going to move anytime soon.

"How about a game of tag? Catch me if you can, Banner! I'll let you have a little bit of fun before you perish!" Caspian cackled, and before Sabrina could make any move to attack, he disappeared in front of Sabrina's eyes.

"Sabrina! Don't get confused! Every sorcerer cloak has its own special power. Caspian's cloak has the magic of invisibility. He can keep himself hidden from sight, hiding like a coward!" Sabrina's dad said.

Sabrina licks her dry lips.

She didn't know where Caspian had gone, but the pathway that she needs to use to get out of the cell had been cleared. Sabrina heard footsteps running out of the cell, which gave her a little relief. At least Caspian wasn't invisible *and* silent.

She squeezed her eyes shut and listened for footsteps, breathing, or anything that could help her figure out where Caspian was standing.

Everything and everyone was completely silent.

Frederick and Aureum probably thought that she'd lost it, but Sabrina knew better.

She had no clue how cloaks worked or how sorcerers got their cloaks, but now she knew that each cloak had its own special power.

Caspian's was invisibility, as she had just learned. Sabrina subconsciously held her breath, knowing that Caspian could strike at any moment.

Any second.

That was what Sabrina despised the most.

She needed to stay collected and focused.

"Caspian, where are you?!" Sabrina screamed.

She had no idea how big his secret cave hideout was, but she did know that the cell that she had been trapped in had a doorway that was wide open. Taking advantage of it, Sabrina stepped out of the cell, only to be greeted by a pair of hallways that went two different directions. "Come out and fight me, you coward!" she yelled.

Sabrina could feel her whole body trembling, and the only sound in the room was Sabrina's unsteady and nervous breathing.

Then without warning, Sabrina felt her whole body freeze up, and she found herself unable to move. She was slowly lifted into the air and turned around to face Caspian.

He looked at her with hatred in his one good eye, and a bony hand was outstretched in front of him, red magic flowing from it.

As much as Sabrina could, she looked down at her hands and notices the red magic around her body, like an aura.

"Hello, Sabrina. Miss me?" Caspian murmured in a bone-chilling whisper.

"Um, how can I miss you when I literally just met you?" Sabrina said, letting out a shaky breath.

"How rude!" Caspian exclaimed, and Sabrina simply shrugged. Caspian glared at her before saying, "Well, this was fun and all, Miss Banner, but now you lose. Game over." Caspian clenched his outstretched hand into a fist.

Sabrina choked, realizing that his hand controlled the red magic around her. His hand was currently her life force.

The more he squeezed it, the more air she lost and the faster she died.

Her life was in his hands. Sabrina felt so weak and defenseless.

How could she fight when she had no control over her body?

How could she do anything when her fate was in Caspian's hands?

Then a thought struck her.

She could try to buy herself some more time.

Maybe, just maybe, she could talk a little sense into the crazy psychopath who was currently choking her to death, keeping her suspended in midair, frozen and unable to move. He was teasing her, loosening and tightening his grip on his clenched fist, giving and taking away her air.

Sabrina knew what she had to do.

She wasn't completely helpless.

Not yet.

She could still win.

She could outsmart him.

"Why?" Sabrina managed to ask, struggling for air and feeling tears form in her eyes as she kept fighting against Caspian.

"Why, what?" Caspian challenged, acting careless, but Sabrina could hear the curiosity in his voice.

"Why are you doing this? Why do you want eternal life? Where's the glory in that? Eventually, everything and everyone will die. So what's the point of living forever?" Sabrina asked between gasps of breath.

"Because, Miss Sabrina," Caspian began, a smirk forming on his lips. "When one realm dies, I've got tons of others to take over and rule. I'll never be forgotten. I'll be remembered by all, feared by all. I'll be the most powerful and the strongest. I'll have access to everything, and I'll have people to do my dirty work. I'll get revenge on the people who turned their backs on me. Revenge on those who trapped me in one realm, and then another."

"Revenge? Revenge on whom?" Sabrina pressed; hoping to hit a nerve and feeling Caspian loosen his clenched fist slightly.

But then Sabrina's hope faltered moment as Caspian tightened his grasp again, fury on his face. "Revenge on Angelica. She took everything from me! I had the realms in my grasp. I was so close! Years ago, I could have succeeded in total realm domination, but she caused my downfall!" Caspian screeched, and he stomped his foot.

If Sabrina weren't trying to keep herself alive, she might have even laughed at Caspian's childish behavior. "Ruling over all of the realms was my right. And it still is. It's my destiny. We both have destinies, Sabrina Banner. But I was supposed to rule! I was supposed to conquer!" Caspian screamed again, and Sabrina winced as she felt herself losing more air.

"Let my daughter go, Caspian!" Fred yelled furiously.

"Be quiet, Frederick! I'm not done yet!" Caspian hollered back.

Sabrina felt herself growing tired, and she suddenly wanted nothing more than to close her eyes and sleep. It would be much easier to give in and let herself fall asleep.

But falling asleep would mean sleeping forever, never waking up again, and Sabrina knew that it would be selfish.

"I'm going to enjoy killing you. I've been hunting you for fifteen painstaking years," Caspian continued, and he gave a dry, cold-hearted laugh. "My Nightshades delivered you to me, just as I created them to do. It took them much longer than I had anticipated, but no matter. Here we are now, just moments away from my victory, thanks to Sylvester." Caspian cackled, and Sabrina felt her blood run cold.

Sylvester has been in on this?

He helped Caspian capture me?

What?

"Soon I shall rule and have my revenge. But until then, I'm going to enjoy watching you suffer and slowly die, Sabrina Banner. Right in front of your father's eyes. Angelica thought that she had won, but she had only postponed my unavoidable destiny. I will not suffer for the rest of my days as she had intended. I will not wither away into nothing and be forgotten. That is not my destiny!" Caspian shook with anger, his teeth gritted and his fist tightly clenched.

Sabrina felt herself letting go.

It made her feel so weak and like a failure.

She hadn't even come close to defeating Caspian.

She was going to die as a disappointment.

"I may have lost some of my sanity in the process, but it's not my fault!" Caspian bellowed. "It's was all Angelica's fault! She turned me into what everyone fears! She made me the villain and altered my fate! All because I was different, more powerful than her, and she knew it! That's why she put me here! Because Angelica was a coward and knew that she was too weak to defeat me! She died a cowardly death to save herself from facing my wrath, and she will live with the guilt of it for the rest of her life. And I will win!" Caspian said, his voice dropping to a dangerous whisper.

But Sabrina felt something for the man in front of her that she didn't expect herself to ever feel, especially after his very long rant.

She felt pity.

Caspian clearly had abandonment issues and the fear of being forgotten.

Oddly enough, Sabrina could feel that Caspian was just as terrified about whatever was to come as she was.

Maybe it was the delusion taking over from the lack of oxygen.

But whatever it was, it helped Sabrina see past his cold, guarded exterior.

"You don't have to be this way," Sabrina forced herself to gasp out, having almost no strength left to speak.

The very least she could do before she died was to try to reason with Caspian, make some sort of peace.

"*Pardon?*" Caspian remarked, his anger faltering and his clenched fist loosening.

Sabrina greedily took a second to get some more air before continuing. "Angelica didn't fear you, Caspian. No one does. No one thought you to be the villain. You became one yourself, by the choices that you made. But you can change it. As cheesy as this sounds, your fate isn't set in stone," Sabrina said slowly as the ancient prophecy recited itself in her head.

"Like you, everyone thinks my fate to be already decided. But I'm not going to let it be that way. You don't have to let it be that way either. You became this way because you didn't—"

Sabrina suddenly found herself choking, and she noticed Caspian tightening his grip. "Because I didn't, what?" he snarled.

"You didn't fight!" Sabrina screamed, gasping for air.

Caspian looked at Sabrina, almost forgetting that he was holding her in a choke hold as he analyzed her face with curiosity.

"You sound just like everyone else," Caspian scoffed.

Then Sabrina realized something.

He wasn't clenching his fist as tightly anymore.

It was almost as if he had forgotten, and the red magic around her had weakened its hold.

She could wiggle her fingers and toes without a problem.

Her plan was working.

Caspian seemed lost in thought for a moment, slightly taken aback, and Sabrina was released from being suspended in midair as well as becoming completely unfrozen.

She fell to the ground and grunted from the sudden pain, but she managed a sigh of relief, knowing that she had made him second-guess himself.

"Sabrina!" Fred called with concern after seeing Sabrina fall to the floor like that.

"I'm fine, Dad!" Sabrina reassured him, even though she felt the exact opposite of fine. Her throat was killing her as she struggled to catch her breath, and her joints felt stiff after being restricted from movement.

"Sabrina, move!" Fred suddenly cried.

"Sabrina, look out!" Aureum exclaimed in panic.

Sabrina was pulled from her thoughts and yanked back into reality when Caspian launched a ball of magic toward her.

She ducked and barely dodging it.

She thought that she had gotten through to him, but clearly not.

Instead, Sabrina had only bought herself some more time.

She could feel her heart hammering against her chest as fear crept upon her. Adrenaline rushed through Sabrina's body, keeping her on her feet.

Sabrina racked her brain to remember something as Caspian continued to throw enchanted flames, spells, and balls of magic at her.

Sabrina needed to remember something, anything from the book of spells that Aureum had showed her.

Think, Sabrina.

Think!

Her eyebrows furrowed together in frustration and determination as she continued to dodge Caspian's attacks.

Then Sabrina heard the sound of footsteps a few feet off to her right. She needed to catch Caspian by surprise. She needed to use a spell. She needed to use magic.

Fortunately for her, something in her brain clicked, and Sabrina conveniently remembered the spell that Professor Angus had tried to teach her. Aureum had helped her learn it better. Sabrina knew how to create fire in the palm of her hand.

Sabrina stuck out her hand, her palm facing upward, and she murmured the spell under her breath in Bermuda as best as she could remember.

"Elprup Erif!" Sabrina said, casting the spell.

Sabrina was unfortunately greeted with a small purple flame forming in her hand, much to her disappointment.

She grunted in frustration but decided that it was better than nothing.

She tossed the little flame toward Caspian but missed, leaving Caspian looking amused. Sabrina growled angrily.

Caspian burst into laughter, clutching his stomach and wiping a tear from his eye.

"That was hilarious, my dear child! But really useless. The little pep talk was cute, and congratulations on striking a nerve, making me feel emotions. But it's going to take a lot more than that to defeat me! *Just give up!* You're only buying yourself a little more time before you meet your doom!"

Sabrina was breathing heavily, anger, fear, helplessness, and despair bubbling up inside of her.

"Sabrina, he's toying with you! Don't listen to him!" Aureum called out to Sabrina.

Sabrina wanted to believe Aureum.

She knew that her friend was right, but she couldn't help but think that

Caspian wasn't bluffing. Sabrina turned her attention back to Caspian, who smirked, and his eyes held an evil gleam.

Sabrina gasped in fright.

Caspian summoned magic to conjure a weapon in his hand.

It was shaped like a long scythe that had a golden aura glow around it. It reminded Sabrina of the grim reaper.

"Fight me, Sabrina! Create a weapon of your own, and we'll fight." Caspian sneered.

"Come again?" Sabrina squeaked, feeling helpless and small in comparison to Caspian.

How am I supposed to make a weapon out of thin air?

I can hardly remember spells that Aureum taught me!

What makes him think that I'm capable of creating a weapon out of magic?

I'm dead.

So dead!

Sabrina thought in despair.

"Go on. Create a weapon, girl," Caspian challenged, obviously feeling victorious about whatever was to come next.

Sabrina let out a shaky breath.

Create a weapon.

Yeah, I can totally do that.

Maybe.

Or not.

"Sabrina!" Aureum's voice rang out, bringing Sabrina back into reality. "Imagine a weapon of your choice forming in your hands. Conjure all of the magic in you and pull it together to create what you want!"

"What? Isn't that impossible?" Sabrina asked, feeling hopeless.

"Just listen to me, and—look out!" Aureum screeched.

Despite Sabrina's confusion, she turned just in time as Caspian swung his scythe over her head. Sabrina yelped and managed to duck just in time. Her heart raced again.

Create a weapon …

Create a weapon …

Come on, Sabrina.

Create a weapon!

After sucking in a breath, Sabrina focused on every ounce of magic flowing through her veins. She held out her hand and kept avoiding Caspian's strikes. Sabrina focused on creating a weapon.

This was not a fair fight.

But then again, when are fights ever fair?

Sabrina mustered up all of her strength to construct a weapon out of magic.

Then there was a blinding flash that threw both Caspian and Sabrina off guard. When the light died down, Sabrina gasped, and her jaw dropped at the sight of the weapon that had formed in her grasp: a long bronze sword with a golden glow and a leather hilt was in her dominant left hand.

"*Impossible,*" Caspian breathed, seeming to be just as awestruck as Sabrina was.

The room was in dead silence. No one uttered a single word.

Then Sabrina's dad broke the silence. "The Sword of a Half-Blood," he murmured.

"The Sword of what?" Sabrina asked, turning her attention from her new sword to her dad in confusion.

"The Sword of a Half-Blood," Caspian spat. "A very rare sword that only can be made by a … well, a half-blood, which is what you are. You have the soul of two inside of you, not making you as full as one. You're only half of each. The sword hasn't been seen for eons, but it seems that your magic called upon it to be summoned. I'll admit, Banner, I'm impressed. But the odds are still in my favor. You still stand no chance again me."

Before Sabrina could retort, Caspian launched himself at her. Out of instinct, Sabrina swung her new sword at him, blocking the hit of his scythe.

That was how they went for quite a while.

Caspian kept slashing at Sabrina with his scythe, and she kept fighting back with her sword. Sabrina was surprised that it fit so perfectly in her grasp.

It wasn't too heavy or too small.

It was as if it had been made just for her. Sabrina had no clue how to use the sword or how to fight properly, and so she dodged and blocked Caspian's hits as much as she could.

She soon found herself growing tired again.

She wished that she could remember more of the spells that Aureum had tried to teach her, but because she couldn't fully understand or read Bermuda, it was difficult for her to remember the spells and symbols.

Caspian swung at Sabrina again, and she dodged it, slipping past him and turning the battle around so he was in the cell and Sabrina was in the stone hallway. Caspian was fuming. "Silly little girl. You still think you can win?" he said, trying to not show how angry and frustrated he was.

"Actually ... yes, I do," Sabrina replied, sounding more confident than she felt.

"And what makes you think that?" Caspian snarled as he threw himself at Sabrina again. Sabrina grunted as their weapons made contact.

The sound of the metal connecting echoed off the walls.

"Because you wouldn't be trying to distract me with talking unless you feared defeat," Sabrina retorted, feeling a little spark of hope forming in her. Despite feeling slightly more confident, she told herself to not get cocky.

When you get cocky, that's when things go wrong and people get hurt.

Caspian growled and came at Sabrina in a whirlwind. He swung and stabbed his scythe at her. Fury burned in his cold eyes. "I will not be defeated by a little mere mortal! You're just a child! Who cares if you happen to be part sorcerer! You will be the final ingredient to the incantation! I will live for eternally and rule over all!"

Then suddenly the ground shook, knocking both of them temporarily off balance. Sabrina placed a hand on the stone wall to keep herself from face planting.

"What was that?" Aureum squeaked.

Sabrina could tell that Aureum was freaking out and wishing that she wasn't frozen in spot.

"Whatever it is, it doesn't affect me. I'm sure it was nothing," Caspian replied carelessly. Then he threw himself at Sabrina, and they were at it again.

The ground stopped shaking only long enough for Sabrina to catch her breath. Then it started trembling, causing rocks from the ceiling to fall and the walls to slightly crack. Was there a mini earthquake going on outside?

Whatever it was, Sabrina didn't like it.

It kept knocking her off of her feet, giving Caspian the upper hand. Out of the blue, Sabrina's cloak took control of the battle and yanked Sabrina out of the way of Caspian's scythe. "Thank you," she murmured quietly to her cloak, suddenly finding a reason to like it.

If it hadn't just done that, she would have been hit with Caspian's scythe and would likely be dead.

Caspian muttered curses under his breath before yelling, "You will perish, girl!"

This reminded Sabrina of every fantasy book that she'd ever read.

The villain got all cocky, and everyone thought he was going to win.

Everyone thought that all hope was lost.

But then miraculously the heroine or hero pulled some crazy stunt and managed to defeat the villain. So if that was what happened in every fantasy book and battle, where was Sabrina's new, cool move that would help her win?

She was the good guy, right?

Good guys always won, so why was Sabrina having such a hard time defeating Caspian?

What did he have that she didn't?

The answer to that was simple: more experience. He knew what he was doing. He'd been doing it for years.

Meanwhile, Sabrina had just learned about all of this no more than three days ago. Then she'd taken this secret quest to take him down, still not having mastered any magic.

Yet here Sabrina was, still fighting him.

Sabrina didn't know how this battle would turn out, but she did know that the odds were beyond scary.

Caspian smiled coldly, and it sent shivers down Sabrina's spine.

He had a look on his face that said, *'I know something that you don't'* and to be honest, it scared Sabrina.

Suddenly Caspian had Sabrina backed up against the wall.

Sabrina had been so lost in her thoughts that she hadn't been paying attention to the battle. She mentally cursed herself, for the millionth time, for getting so easily distracted. Caspian held his scythe to her neck, and she glared at him.

"This has been fun and all, my dear, but I think it's time for a new king to rise. A new era. My golden era. Any last words?" Caspian had a wicked, twisted expression on his lips. This man was absolutely mad!

"Think for a second, Caspian!" Sabrina cried, trying to hit a nerve again.

"Eternal life? Is that really what you want? What's so good about living forever? You lose everyone and everything that you've ever cared about. Admit it or not, but I know that there's at least someone or something that you care about in this world and in the realms, besides wanting to rule all of them! Consider it, at the very least! You'll live with the guilt of killing people! You'll regret it after it's done, and once it is done, there's no going back." Sabrina let out a shaky breath. She couldn't keep this up forever. She knew that the chances of convincing him were slim.

"I never regret anything, Sabrina Banner. I've lived a painful life. I've suffered long enough. It's time for me to receive what's mine. I shall finally have my reward. And I—"

Caspian was cut off when the ground shook again and more rocks toppled from the ceiling. One hit Caspian in the head.

He yelped in pain and lowered his scythe to tend to his bleeding wound. Sabrina took this opportunity to kick him in the stomach and get out of his grasp.

The ground wouldn't stop shaking this time. Sabrina needed to save Aureum, Chi, and her dad and get out of here, regardless of whether it meant defeating Caspian.

Ignoring Caspian, Sabrina turned around and dashed back into the cell, where Aureum and her dad still remained frozen, the purple aura trapping them in place.

"Aureum, this place isn't going to hold up for much longer. How can I get you both out?" Sabrina asked frantically.

"There's a spell you can use to free us, Sabrina! I know the spell, but the one being held can't use it. Only someone who's standing by can recite the spell and have it work," Aureum explained.

"Okay, so what's the spell?" Sabrina said with panic in her voice.

Aureum recited the spell for Sabrina, and despite the tricky pronunciation, Sabrina managed to say it mostly correctly.

The aura that had held Aureum, Chi, and Frederick in place disappeared.

Aureum fell to her knees, and Frederick groaned.

"Aureum, are you okay?" Sabrina asked worriedly as she helped the girl back to her feet.

"Yeah. It's just … ow. My muscles are sore." She winced and stretched her arms.

"Dad, what about you? Are you all right?" Sabrina asked, turning her attention to her dad.

"Yes, I'm—Sabrina, look out!" Fred cried.

Sabrina quickly turned around, but it was too late.

The last thing Sabrina saw was Caspian launching his scythe at her, and it hit her in her stomach. Everything seemed to turn black and white and go in slow motion.

"Enjoy the Astro Realm," Caspian hissed, and before her world went dark, the last thing Sabrina remembered was her dad and Aureum letting out panicked cries.

Then there was a bright, blinding light.

X. "Unfinished Business"

Sabrina's body felt heavy and yet weightless at the same time. She felt as though she was being suspended in midair.

She groggily opened her eyes, feeling exhausted, as if all of the energy had been drained out of her. The first thing that Sabrina noticed when she regained consciousness was that she was floating. The world around her reminded her of a nebula in outer space.

Despite floating, Sabrina's body felt heavy, as if gravity didn't want her to float and was trying to push her back to the ground.

She felt torn between falling and floating. Sabrina forced herself up from floating on her belly to an upright position, struggled to keep upright.

"Where am I?" Sabrina mumbled aloud.

She took in her surroundings.

It was as if she had been swallowed by a little galaxy. Everything around her was like the night sky, with random swirls of color almost like the Northern Lights, and with a million little stars encircling her. Before Sabrina knew it, she was free falling.

She tried to scream, but her voice was caught in her throat.

Everything flew past her at a crazy speed.

The colors of the sky mashed together, making Sabrina's head spin.

Then suddenly, a bright light came into view. Sabrina kept silently screaming, and she squeezed her eyes shut, hoping that this wasn't the end.

The next thing she knew, she was lying on the white floor of a balcony that overlooked the empty galactic void. Sabrina groaned and made herself sit up, oddly not feeling any pain as she had expected.

Sabrina's heart raced as she took in everything around her.

It was all so strange.

She managed to push herself up to her feet as she slowly spun around, taking in her surroundings.

She gasped and walked backwards as she looked up at the big structure behind her. It was a giant white castle, and it seemed to be never ending in height.

"Whoa," she said in awe. "Where is this place?" She then glanced down at her attire and gasped again. She notices that she was no longer in her pajamas. Instead, she wore an elegant white dress with gold designs throughout it and golden sandals on her feet.

"This is so weird," Sabrina muttered to herself feeling utterly confused. "Hello?"

Sabrina walked back over to the balcony and looked over the golden railing, into the empty void. Sabrina suddenly noticed out of the corner of her eyes that her hands were practically translucent. It was like she was a ghost or something. She could almost see through them.

Sabrina gulped, fearing the worst.

Am I dead?

Did … did Caspian kill me?

What was the last thing that happened?

How did I get here?

Question upon question piled up in Sabrina's head as she desperately racked her brain to remember what had happened.

Everything that had recently happened seemed to be a blur. But then realization dawned on Sabrina as the recent events surfaced.

Caspian and Sabrina had been fighting, scythe against sword. Caspian's little makeshift hideout in the Bermuda Triangle had been in some cave, made out of stone, and it was beginning to crumble.

Sabrina had been trying to free her dad and Aureum. She had managed to do so, but when she turned around, Caspian had stabbed Sabrina with his scythe.

Did that mean that she was dead?

"No, my dear child. You are not dead—but you are dying."

Sabrina let out a yelp of surprise when her eyes landed on a woman floating toward her. The woman was tall.

Her body was translucent like Sabrina's, and she wore a flowing white dress with straps that hung loosely on her shoulders.

The woman's hair was pulled back into an elegant bun with a crown of golden leaves placed upon her head.

"Who are you? Did you just read my thoughts? And how am I not dead? I got stabbed. I should be dead. There's no possible way that I could still be alive. And where am I? And—"

"Silence, child. Maybe if you stop talking and give me a chance to speak, your questions will be answered."

The woman spoke softly in a way that reminded Sabrina of Aureum. Sabrina nodded slowly, allowing the woman to speak.

"My name is Angelica Henry."

Sabrina's jaw dropped.

She should've known that.

Professor Linus had taken her class on a tour to a hallway of the Academy, where they had walked past a portrait of Angelica Henry, the headmistress of the Academy before Amaris.

Angelica smiled. "Correct. I see you're caught up on your history, which is a surprise, considering that you only went to the Academy for a day." Sabrina opens her mouth to ask a question, but Angelica cut her off.

"And yes, I am reading your thoughts, Sabrina Banner. It's an ability of that you receive in the Astro Realm. Do not question it further, please; I wish not to speak of it. But nonetheless, we must move on quickly. You do not have much time. When Caspian stabbed you, he only killed one of your two souls—your sorcerer's soul. Any magic that you could've had is now gone, and you are only mortal."

Sabrina eyes got big in surprise.

I don't have any more magic?

So I was tossed into this world, only to be killed and be deprived of any possible magic I could've had? She felt angry and confused.

"Please, Sabrina. I know you're surprised, shocked, and angry, but it's the truth. You are now purely mortal. Without your sorcerer's soul, you would've died completely. Your sorcerer's soul acted as armor around your mortal soul and took the blow of Caspian's magical scythe. Your friend, Aureum, has to make a decision: to save you or leave you. There is a spell that she can use to bring you back to life, but it's a dangerous spell that should almost never be tampered with. She doesn't have much time to choose, but I pray she will choose correctly and save you. If not, then if time does run out, your soul will be forever trapped here in the Astro Realm, a place where the spirit is separate from the body."

This was so much to take in all at once. Sabrina placed a hand to her head and squeezed her eyes shut.

"So … So you're saying that Aureum can either bring me back to life or leave me to die? And why do you want her to let me live?" She hadn't meant for it to sound rude, but she didn't have any patience left.

Angelica let out a small sigh but nodded. "Yes. It's up to Aureum, because she and your father are still in Caspian's hideout. It's still crumbling, but they need to choose. And if they don't bring you back, everything goes to loss. The prophecy will be useless, and the other sorcerers won't stand a chance against the upcoming war."

Sabrina paled. *"Upcoming war?"*

"Yes," Angelica said. "An upcoming war. Right after Caspian stabbed you, he managed to use a spell to flash himself out of his hideout, but your friend and father were too distressed to do anything."

"How do you know all of this?" Sabrina asked.

Angelica let out a deep breath. "I have a way of being able to see into other realms from this one. When you die, if you are someone who has unfinished business, you get sent here. Once you've completed it, you're free to choose between rebirth or going to heaven. Being able to see into other realms is part of what will help you with your unfinished business," she answered grimly.

"So you're here because of unfinished business? What's your unfinished business? And why am I here?" Sabrina asked.

She hated not knowing.

She had questions upon questions.

One answer simply led to another question.

"I made a promise that I would do what I can to help the prophecy child. I cannot go to rest until the child of the prophecy has either failed or completed the task."

Sabrina felt a weird feeling fill up in her stomach—and it was not a good feeling.

"Don't worry, Sabrina. I chose this path. I'm glad the child is you.

I have a good feeling about the future. For all I knew when I made the promise, I could've been stuck here for eons, waiting for the savor. But now you're here, which leads to your unfinished business. You're either going to complete or fail the prophecy. After one or the other is completed, when you die, your spirit, or soul, is put to rest." Angelica ended on a grim note.

Sabrina swallowed and ran a hand through her hair. "This is crazy! My whole life was already planned out before I was even born. So much for it not being written in stone," she grumbled, crossing her arms.

Changing the subject, Angelica said, "I see my cloak found a new master."

Sabrina glanced down at the shimmery dark blue cloak with the golden trim that she was wearing and smiled sheepishly. "Um, yeah. Funny story, actually, with how it chose me ..." she voice trailed off awkwardly.

Angelica smiled faintly. "It's fine." She waved her hand in dismissal. "Ever since you arrived at the Academy, I've been watching you. Being born of two souls, I knew that you obviously weren't normal. I knew that you could possibly be the savor we've been waiting for, and so I took no chances."

Sabrina blushed, feeling slightly weird that Angelica had been watching her for four days now. "I do not mean that to sound weird or strange, Sabrina. But I had to make sure you were on the right track, and it seems to me that you were."

To be honest, Sabrina did feel a little better.

Suddenly, a sharp pain exploded in her head, and she doubled over, squeezing her eyes shut and clutching her head. It was like a really bad migraine. Sabrina let out a groan of pain as she felt Angelica place a hand on her shoulder.

"Aureum chose correctly! She chose to save you. Here, take my ring, Sabrina, it was my Realm Traveling Device." Angelica slid a ring with a golden band and a teal gem off of her finger and placed it in Sabrina's hand. "Your father will know how it works. I know about Aureum's belt, but just in case anything goes wrong, you now have the ring. I wish you the best of luck. And please promise me that you won't give up. I know this is hard, but if you don't prevail, everything will crumble and parish."

Sabrina laughed dryly. "So no pressure. Right," she said bitterly.

Angelica looked at her sympathetically. "I'm sorry, Sabrina. But I have faith in you. Remember, I'll be watching you from here. You'll do great things, I'm sure of it. Good luck."

Angelica was saying something else, but Sabrina's head was pounding too much for her to focus on the words. Sabrina's vision blurred, and her knees gave out. Before Sabrina knew it, once again Sabrina's world tumbled into an abyss of never-ending darkness.

"—ina! Sabrina? Sabrina? Please, wake up!"

Sabrina heard a faint voice frantically crying. Sabrina's eyelids felt heavy. All she wanted to do was sleep.

"Sabrina, you're alive! Thank goodness! Aureum, get your belt ready. I'll carry Sabrina," she heard another voice say. Sabrina's head was pounding, and she couldn't make out who was who, or who was saying what. Sabrina could hear the blood rushing in her ears. She groaned as she felt someone pick her up.

"It's okay, Sabrina. I've got you," a voice said soothingly to Sabrina. She wishes that she could have replied or given the person some sign that she was all right. But before Sabrina could do anything else, there was a blinding flash, and once again the world faded before her eyes as she lost consciousness yet again.

Sabrina rolled underneath soft, thin, brown bed sheets on a hard cot. Her brain instantly picked up on where she was, even before opening her eyes. Even though she had only been there once, Sabrina knew that she was back at the Academy, in the infirmary.

Is this how it's going to be every time I realm travel?

Waking up in the infirmary? Apparently so, Sabrina thought with slight annoyance.

A small groan escaped her lips as she groggily opened her eyes. A blinding light splashed onto Sabrina's face, causing her to grunt as she flipped herself over onto her stomach, where she then buried her face into the pillow, trying to block out the blinding light.

"Sabrina?" her dad's voice rang out from somewhere to her right.

Sabrina groaned her again and mumbled, "What?"

He chuckled softly. "You gave us quite a scare. I'm glad you're alive."

Sabrina turned over on her back again and frowned, looking her dad in the eyes.

He looked exhausted and sat in a chair beside Sabrina's bed, reminding her of when she'd first come to the Sorcerer Realm with Sylvester.

Sabrina's heart ached slightly at the thought of Sylvester, and she momentarily wondered what had happened to him, but she quickly pushed aside the feeling.

"But I did die. And then Aureum brought me back to life," Sabrina said in a quiet and tired voice.

Her dad's eyes widened. "How did you—"

"Know that?" Sabrina finished, and he nodded slowly.

Sabrina exhaled deeply and slowly pushed herself up into a sitting position. Her dad helped her sit up and put some pillows behind her back so that she didn't have to use much energy to sit up.

"After Caspian stabbed me, I … I went to the Astro Realm," Sabrina said as she watched her dad's facial expression change to surprise.

"You did? But … but that's only for—"

"Souls with unfinished business. I know. But my business is—er, was, unfinished," Sabrina corrected herself.

Her dad listened intently, taking everything in and allowing his brain to process it all.

"When I woke up there, Angelica Henry's spirit greeted me."

Her dad opened his mouth to speak, but Sabrina kept talking before he could get a word in. "And yes, *the* Angelica Henry, as in the headmistress before Amaris. Anyways, she explained to me what happened and where I was. She told me that when Caspian killed me, I lost one of my souls. I lost my sorcerer's soul."

"The one that your magic comes from," Dad interrupted.

Sabrina nodded. "Yeah. Which kind of sucks, but that's beside the point. Anyway, she told me you guys were still in Caspian's little hideout, and Aureum had to make a choice to either save me or let me die. Angelica wanted Aureum to save me. She told me that I still had to complete the prophecy, and if I didn't, I'd be trapped in the Astro Realm. Fortunately for the both of us, Aureum obviously chose to save me." Sabrina gestured to herself with her hands, and her dad cracked a small smile.

After letting out a breath, Sabrina winced slightly from the pain in her stomach before ignoring it and continuing. "That means I still have a chance of defeating Caspian. And yes, I know he was a coward and disappeared after he stabbed me. Before I woke up back at Caspian's hideout with you guys, Angelica gave me her ring."

Sabrina held out her hand so that her dad could see the ring that sat on her right ring finger. He studied it with awe.

"That ... that was Angelica's realm traveling Device. So not only do you have her cloak, but you also have her realm traveling device. She must really trust you." He gave a proud smile.

Sabrina forced a small smile in return. "Um, yeah. Well, the only reason that she trusts me is because I'm the reason why she's in the Astro Realm," she said quietly.

Her dad frowned and raised an eyebrow. "Sabrina, you weren't even alive when she died."

"Yeah, I know. But Angelica promised she would watch over the prophecy child, and she can't be put to rest until the prophecy is completed, whether I fail or prevail."

Her Dad was about to speak, but they're interrupted by none other than Amaris Nightingale. "Ah, Sabrina. I'm pleased to see that you are awake. Oh, and the rumors are true. Hello, Frederick." Amaris spoke with such an emotionless tone, and she stood with poise, her hands folded neatly behind her.

She turned her head, and Sabrina looked where she was looking to see Sage standing beside her, fidgeting with the bottom of his shirt.

"Thank you for leading me here, Sage. You can go," Amaris commanded.

Sage nodded and smiled weakly at Sabrina before turning on his heels and leaving the trio alone.

"Amaris," Sabrina's dad said. Sabrina couldn't tell what he was feeling. His face was blank, and his voice held no emotion.

"Frederick." Amaris kept the same tone. "I thought you were dead. You disappear for years, and now you're magically alive. Not to mention that your daughter is the prophecy child and Sylvester is dead." She laughed dryly. "Sounds pretty messed up, doesn't it?"

Sabrina swallowed hardly. "So he's ... he's actually gone?" she asked quietly.

Amaris and Frederick both glanced at her, her dad with sympathy.

"Yes. Or at least, we assume him to be," Dad replied softly.

Sabrina let her shoulders slump as everything around her seemed to crumble. "I ... I can't—" She squeezed her eyes shut. "No ..." Her voice trembled.

She felt a rough hand place itself on her shoulder and squeeze it comfortingly.

"I know. I can't believe it either. But it happened, and we have to let him go," her dad said gently.

Sabrina nodded and let out a breath before reopening her eyes and then drying them before tears could spill.

"Anyway, as tragic as this news is, we must move on. Tomorrow we'll—"

"Wait! What's tomorrow's date?" Sabrina screeched, ignoring the pain that she felt on her stomach from moving quickly.

"Tomorrow? Um ... Amaris, what is tomorrow's date? I haven't had access to anything that tells time lately ..." Frederick's voice trailed off.

Amaris sighed in annoyance. "Tomorrow is March 23."

"March 23?" Sabrina interrupted, causing those around her to wince at her loud voice.

Sabrina blushed from embarrassment before shaking her head and recomposing herself. "I need to be home in two days from now. My spring break is almost over. Amaris, please, please let me go home tomorrow. I can't stay here forever. I have no reason to stay. Dad and I can return to the Mortal Realm. My aunt, cousin, and friends are expecting me. Please let me go home. I have no magic left. My Sorcerer's Soul is gone. If you want me to, I swear I'll come back," Sabrina pleaded.

Amaris looked taken aback but she quickly recomposed herself.

"Sabrina, I simply cannot allow you to—"

"Amaris, let us go. You don't want me here anyway. I'm not allowed to stay here. I got expelled, remember? Besides that, I can protect Sabrina. She still has to defeat Caspian, yes. But like she said, she's currently powerless. Fully Mortal. And she's right: what purpose does she have left here? A non-magic sorcerer at a school full of people with magic. That sounds ridiculous. We'll come back, but for now, let Sabrina enjoy life. Her life was planned out by an ancient prophecy. Let her settle for a little while, and we'll think of how else to defeat Caspian without magic. I'm sure there's a way. But please, Amaris, be reasonable."

For a second, Sabrina saw Amaris's expression soften as her Dad spoke. It was almost sympathetic.

Amaris exhaled in defeat. "All right, fine," she said, waving her hands around as she talked. "You two can go home. But Sabrina, I want you back here every chance you have. Take a break, if you wish, but I know mortals have a thing called *summer*. When that comes around, come back here unless plans change. You may not have magic, but according to the prophecy, you are still the one who has to take down Caspian. Remember the prophecy?"

"Of course. It's kind of engraved into my head." Sabrina closed her eyes and recited it. *"Born of mortal blood with magic in her veins, the daughter of a legend will soon begin her reign. She will journey far to seek what has been lost, but she will not return without a high cost. Betrayed by one she called friend, she will battle to the death, until the end."*

"Some of it has already been completed," Sabrina's dad chimed in.

"How so?" Sabrina asked as she turned to him.

She looked like she trying to hide her confusion.

"Well, for starters, you were betrayed by Sylvester, and you called him *friend*, correct?" Sabrina's dad said, not bothering to sugarcoat any of it.

Sabrina nodded, feeling numb at the thought of Sylvester and his betrayal.

"So that part has been fulfilled. The part before says that you won't return without a high cost, and if I'm correct, losing your sorcerer's soul is a high cost. It's going to make winning this battle much more difficult."

Amaris nodded her head in agreement.

"Also you have already technically died, so therefore that part is completed as well. We don't know how the battle will turn out. That's the only part of the prophecy that has yet to be answered," Fred concluded.

Sabrina exhaled deeply and threw her head back onto her pillow, covering her face with her hands. "Why does my life have to suddenly be so complicated? Just days ago, I wished for something more out of my every day, normal life. I felt so cheated, like I had been born into a world where everything was ordinary and nothing extraordinary ever happened.

Now I almost wish to have that life back." Sabrina instantly felt guilty after saying it.

Her dad laughed weakly, without humor.

"I suppose that this my fault, one way or another. But I'll make it up to you somehow."

Sabrina wanted to tell him that it was not his fault, but she couldn't think of any reasons as to why that would not be true.

He was the one who had fallen for Sabrina's mom, who was mortal after all. So instead of saying anything, Sabrina just sighed.

"Well, dinner will be starting soon. Sabrina, I suggest you change out of your pajamas and come join us for one last meal before you leave," Amaris stated.

Sabrina uncovered her face and glanced down at her attire. Sure enough, she was still in her purple pajamas with dark blue polka dots. She was no longer in the elegant outfit she had been magically dressed in while in the Astro Realm. She blushed and nods. "Um, yeah. Sounds like a plan." She ignored the heat that rose to her cheeks.

"I put your cloak on the coat rack beside your bed, so you can grab it after you've changed," Fred added as he pointed to the coat rack next to her.

"Thanks," Sabrina replied.

"And here's a new uniform," Amaris finished.

She picked up a folded outfit that sat at the foot of the cot, placed the outfit on Sabrina's lap, and then added, "I will see the both of you at dinner. Frederick, you can sleep in an empty dorm tonight, if you wish. I'll give you the number and the key at dinner." Sabrina watched the headmistress leave the somewhat busy infirmary.

Sighing, Sabrina scooped up the clothes, swung her legs over the cot's edge, and got to her feet. "I'll be right back, Dad. Just let me get changed and wash up."

Frederick nodded. "I'll be here waiting. Take your time."

Sabrina smiled faintly and made her way toward the bathroom. She managed to remember where it was from when she'd first come here.

The second Frederick and Sabrina walked into the dining hall, everything stopped.

Everyone who was eating froze, and people who were talking either clamped their mouths shut or stared at the two with their jaws dropped.

Sabrina spotted Aureum sitting next to Fern, and both of them looked at her. Sabrina immediately felt guilty when she saw Aureum, and yet she was relieved at the same time. She felt guilty for the fact that she didn't think of Aureum when she woke up.

I mean, Aureum did save my life, after all.

Sabrina owed Aureum everything now.

Everyone was looking at Sabrina. "Um, hey," Sabrina said with an awkward wave, only to be greeted by continuous silence.

Sabrina shifted uncomfortably on her feet and glanced over at her dad, who was too busy taking in the appearance of the dining hall to notice what was happening.

Sabrina cleared her throat and began to speak, despite the tension. "Right, so, um … I'm back, and I'm just going to go sit down now. So … yeah." She grabbed Fred's wrist and pulled him toward the table where Aureum and Fern sat. She oddly sat herself down between them, and her dad sat across from her. Then Sabrina chewed the inside of her cheek and drummed her fingers on the table's edge.

"Everyone, stop staring and continue eating! Yes, Sabrina and Aureum have returned from their forbidden journey," Amaris stated as she looked at Sabrina and Aureum with a deadly glare.

Aureum shrunk in her seat, heat rising to her cheeks. Sabrina noticed that Chi sat on Aureum's lap and was sleeping soundly.

"And unfortunately, Sylvester Coulson is no longer with us."

That sentence made Sabrina's heart stop. Even though Sabrina hadn't known Sylvester for that long, it still hurt.

Of course she had been already told of his fate, but it didn't stop the denial. Sylvester was a traitor. It hurt to say it, but it was the truth.

Now that Sylvester had revealed his true colors, Sabrina knew.

And now she would have to be much more careful about whom she trusted.

Sylvester must have had been killed during the battle, Sabrina thought. She didn't know the details or the reason why, but he was gone now.

And Frederick Banner is alive.

"After tonight, Fredrick and Sabrina will be heading back to the

Mortal Realm." Gasps rippled across the room, as well as murmurs of confusion and shock. "Silence!" Amaris ordered.

The talking died down.

"Sabrina will still complete the prophecy, but she's going to enjoy her life in the Mortal Realm while she still can. Do not pester or pry into her life or her reasons. We've worked things out, and she will return. Now, without further ado or any other interruptions, please continue to eat. If I hear that any of you are bugging Sabrina, Aureum, or Frederick, there will be consequences." Amaris looked at everyone as she scanned the room, warning everyone with a deadly glare. "And when you're done, we'll gather in the main hall, where our tree decorating will commence and presents will be placed. Of course, if you're new to the Academy, do not fret or worry about the presents. Now, eat up!"

Amaris sat down, and everyone slowly began to eat and talk again.

XI. "The Story of Fred"

For Frederick Banner, the rest of the night went by in a blur.

Fred allowed Sabrina to hang out with her friends.

Aureum had accompanied Sabrina on her quest to rescue him and possibly stop Caspian. Fred didn't know what to think of everything as he aimlessly wandered the Academy's hallways. Memories flashed through his mind, bringing him back to when he'd attended the Academy—before he got expelled.

He had loved the Academy and was probably near the top of his class. Fred missed the old days, before Caspian had captured him and taken so many years away from him. He missed when Angelica had been alive and had been the headmistress.

That was back when Fed had been just learning how to use magic and when he had first befriended Sylvester and Amaris.

Fred suddenly stopped walking, when Sylvester came to his mind. Sylvester was gone for forever now. It made Fred's heart ache at the thought.

It also made Fred contemplate Sylvester's death. None of them actually knew how he had died. During Caspian and Sabrina's battle, he had run off and never returned.

Fred had scanned for any other life forms with magic before he and Aureum had left with Sabrina, but he'd found nothing.

That could only mean that Sylvester had died.

The spell that Fred had used to check for any life sources scanned every known realm. It wouldn't pinpoint a location, but it would inform him about the person's life status. And according to the spell, Sylvester Coulson was deceased.

It seemed so hard for Fred to fathom.

He had trusted Sylvester with his life.

They were supposed to have had each other's backs.

But clearly that was false.

Sylvester had only cared about working for Caspian, behind Fred's back. If that meant forgetting their many years of friendship, then so be it. Suddenly any sympathy that Fred had felt for Sylvester vanished, replaced by anger. He couldn't believe that Sylvester had ditched him like that. Fred sighed in defeat, letting his shoulders slump.

Surely Sylvester had a reason.

Some personal gain from it.

But then again, maybe Sylvester had changed.

After all, Fred hadn't seen him for over fifteen years. Maybe it was a change of perspective. Fred would never know.

Eventually Fred made his way to dorm 13, which according to Amaris was where Sabrina stayed.

Oddly enough, back when Fred was in school, it had been Amaris's dorm, and Amaris had roomed with another person to whom Fred didn't often talk.

Fred exhaled deeply as he used a key that Sabrina had given him to unlock the door.

Fern had the other key, and so Sabrina said that she'd stick with Fern until they decided to go to bed. Fred had obliged and took Sabrina's key so that he had access to the dorm.

After knocking first, Fred got no response, and he assumed that Sabrina and Fern hadn't returned yet.

He let himself inside and closed the door behind him. Fred exhaled deeply as he looked around the room.

There were two twin-sized beds, each with its own nightstand and a chest at the end, and a door that led to the bathroom in between them.

Fred assumed that the less decorated side of the room was Sabrina's, and so he made his way there and sat down on the bed.

Fred closed his eyes and breathed in deeply, calming his nerves and controlling his wild emotions. He let out a shaky breath and reopened his eyes.

Suddenly Fred jumped as the doorknob to the room jiggled and turned. Fred relaxed when he saw Sabrina and her red-headed girl roommate walk in. Sabrina looked exhausted, and Fred couldn't blame her. She had been through a lot within a few days.

"Hey, Dad," Sabrina greeted Fred with a tired smile.

"Hello, Sabrina. And you're Fern, correct?" Fred said, not wanting to confuse the redhead for someone else.

The girl nodded. "Yep, that's me! Fern Archer." She beamed proudly, and Fred smiles slightly.

"I'm going to start to pack my bag, since we're leaving tomorrow at dawn," Sabrina noted as she walked over to the side of her bed to grab her backpack.

"So that's the time that Amaris wants us out, then?" Fred asked as she cleaned out the chest at the end of her bed.

Sabrina nodded. "That's the plan, anyway. Fern and Aureum are going meet up with us before we leave to say goodbye, just to give you the heads-up." Sabrina put folded, unworn uniforms into her backpack.

"All right, sounds good," Fred replied.

"Hey, Sabrina, I promised a friend that I'd meet up with her in a couple minutes, so I'm going to go do that. Okay?" Fern said as she made her way over to the door.

"Yeah, okay. I'll see you later, then," Sabrina answered, and Fern left the room.

Sabrina exhaled deeply as she sat on the floor, putting her belongings into her backpack.

"Is everything okay, Sabrina?" Fred asked, noticing the sudden change in his daughter's mood.

Sabrina shrugged and murmured, "I don't know. It's complicated."

"What's complicated?" Fred pressed, wanting to be a good father and comfort his daughter.

Sabrina shook her head and said, "I guess I'm just a little overwhelmed. There's nothing in the Sorcerer Realm that can help me anymore. My sorcerer's soul is gone. I'm like … half dead." Sabrina shivered at the thought before continuing. "I'm completely mortal now. I'm powerless, which means I need to find a new way to defeat Caspian."

"We'll figure something out, Sabrina. Trust me. I'm sure we will. The prophecy wouldn't exist if there wasn't a way for you to successfully complete it, in my opinion. We simply haven't discovered the way yet, but we will."

"Aureum wants me to stay here. She doesn't want me to leave and thinks that I'll be safer here, which is true. But I have a family back in the Mortal Realm. I promised them I'd come home, and I intend to keep that promise," Sabrina said, clearly conflicted and stressed.

"Aureum's worried for me, as are many others, which makes me feel bad. Sylvester's ... dead. Caspian's still after me. The fate of the realms is resting on my shoulders, and I have no way to stop any of it. I mean, I may not have magic, but I still have my cloak. My cloak that didn't really come in handy during the battle, but I still have it. I don't want to die again—I already experienced it once. And I have Angelica's RTD, but I don't see what good that will do. I know that I have to do what I to stop Caspian and keep myself alive. It seems so impossible."

Fed had no clue about how to console her. He had a lot to learn about being a parent. "Sabrina, if I'm going to be frank, I'm not sure exactly what to say to make you feel better. I'm not sure how this will all play out. But know that I'm so proud of you, and I'll be by your side every step of the way, till the end."

Sabrina smiled faintly.

"Thanks, Dad. Aunt Jeanette and you will get along well with your inspirational speeches." She giggled.

Fred frowned. "*Jeanette*? As in *Jeannette Clark*? Married to *Kevin Clark*? Your mother's sister?" Fred asked, racking his brain to remember.

"Yep, that's right. Mom gave me to Aunt Jeanette before she died. I've been living with Aunt Jeanette and her daughter—my cousin, Paris—for twelve years now, since I was three," Sabrina explained.

"Oh," Fred replied wisely, taking it all in.

Suddenly, a box on Sabrina's nightstand caught Fred's eye. "No way ..." He said, slowly rising to his feet.

"Dad? Dad, are you okay? What's wrong?" she asked in alarm.

Fred didn't respond as he made his way over to the nightstand and picked up the little wood box. "After all these years ..." he murmured, memories flashing in his mind as he sat back down on the bed and studied the little wooden box with golden designs across the top of it. He exhaled deeply and straightened his posture.

"I see you found your mother's box."

Sabrina nodded slowly. "Um, yeah. Aunt Jeanette gave it to me, actually, before S—" She paused for a moment, not wanting to say Sylvester's name, but she mustered up some courage. *"Sylvester* took me here."

Fred had opened the box and was holding some of the old photos in his hands that Sabrina had seen. With a shaky hand, he gently closed box, squeezed his eyes shut, and let out a shaky breath.

"Dad? Are you okay?" Sabrina asked as she sat down on the bed next to him.

Fred opened his eyes open and smiled at Sabrina sadly. "Yes, Sabrina. I'm okay. I'm just ... *remembering.*"

"Remembering what?" Sabrina pressed, and then she frowned, seeming to regret asking because it was clearly a touchy subject.

"Your mother. My wife. If only she was still here ... Aurora was the most incredible women I have ever met. Perfect in every way, and the love of my life." Fred sighed again and turned to look at Sabrina. His dusty gray eyes met Sabrina's bluish-green ones.

"She'd be so proud of you, Sabrina. You've come so far." He pulled her in for a hug, wrapping his arm over her shoulders, and Sabrina snuggled up against him. "Do you think your aunt will be excited to see me? I only met her once, when I was with Aurora. We got along somewhat well."

"Maybe? I don't know what her thoughts are about you. She never talked about you or Mom much," Sabrina answered truthfully.

Fred laughed at Sabrina's response and planted a fatherly kiss on her head. "Well, if she hasn't changed in the past fifteen years, then she'll probably yell at me so loudly that China can hear. Then she'll slap me, rant, and lecture me for days. Won't that be fun?"

Sabrina smiled faintly at that.

Fred continued. "I can't wait to see Paris. I haven't seen your cousin since you were very little. Paris was three at the time. A small girl she was too, but man, she always spoke what was on her mind. She wasn't afraid to stand up for what she believed in, and that's something big to have at such a young age. The town's probably changed a lot too. I just hope I can adjust."

Fred hugged Sabrina tighter before releasing her and sighing. "Oh, just so you know, Amaris gave me a spare room to sleep in for the night. And since we're leaving early in the morning, be sure to pack up everything tonight. Okay?" Fred said as he got up to his feet.

Sabrina nodded. "Good. I'll see you in the morning, then, Sabrina. And hey ... do you mind, if I take the box with me? I'll give it back. I just want to ..."

"Remember stuff? Yeah, knock yourself out." She smiled at him.

Fred chuckled. "Thank you, Sabrina. I'll see you at dawn, then." He bid her good night before scooping up the wooden box and walking out of her dorm making his way to the spare room that Amaris was letting him use.

That night was rather restless for Fred.

It seemed to last forever, and he didn't sleep very well, maybe for an hour. He spent the remainder of the night lost in thought and remembering.

An hour before they were supposed to leave, Fred got up and headed back to Sabrina's dorm to make sure that she was awake. Sabrina was still sleeping when he got there, so he gently got her to wake up. She was grumpy at first, and Fred couldn't blame her. It was only six thirty in the morning, after all.

"Good morning, Sabrina," Fred murmured to his daughter softly as he gently shook her awake. A groan escaped Sabrina's lips as she buried her face into her pillow and tried to go back to sleep. "Sabrina, it's time to go. According to Aureum, you, and realm traveling don't mix, so we should get a move on."

Sabrina groaned again in response before groggily pushing herself up in bed. She swung her legs over the edge of her bed and rubs her eyes.

Fred smiled at her and said, "Good morning, Sleeping Beauty. Amaris said that Fern, Aureum, and some boy named Sage are here to see us off."

Sabrina frowned at the mention of the last name, and it made Fred question Sabrina's relationship status with the boy. He had no clue as to who Sage was, but he hoped that he and Sabrina had no romantic connection going on.

Sabrina quickly shook off her odd reaction toward the boy and yawned as she trudged over to the chest at the end of her bed, where she grabbed an outfit that had she had prepared the night before. "I'm going to go get dressed," Sabrina informed Fred as she headed into the bathroom of the dorm.

Fred had noticed the Sabrina's redheaded roommate wasn't in the room, and that made him question where she'd be so early in the morning. As he waited, Fred sat back down on Sabrina's bed and thought about how much the Mortal Realm might have changed since he had last visited it.

Eventually, Sabrina returned from the bathroom, no longer in pajamas or wearing an Academy uniform.

She had slipped on a plain light purple T-shirt along, a black sweatshirt, a pair of jeans, and sneakers.

Her messy bed head had been brushed, and Fred took notice of how much Sabrina looks like her mother.

Sabrina had the same short, curly blonde hair as Aurora, and same blue-green eyes.

An uncanny resemblance.

While looking at his daughter's face, he noticed a cut on her bottom lip. He frowned at that, wondering how she had gotten it. Fred decided that it wasn't of importance. Sabrina didn't appear to be in pain or bothered by the cut, and so he let it slide, ignoring his growing curiosity.

"Are you ready to go, Sabrina?" Fred asked as he rose from his spot on her bed.

"In a second. I have to put my cloak in my bag," Sabrina said as she headed over to the coat rack in the corner of the room. Her galaxy-like blue cloak awaited her.

Sabrina smiled as she grabbed the cloak, folded it carefully, and put it in her backpack. "There. Now I'm ready," she declared as she slung her backpack over her shoulders.

Fred nodded. "Excellent. Follow me. Amaris told me to meet her and your friends at the Academy entrance, outside."

"Okay, cool. I haven't been outside of the Academy, aside from Professor Angus's Magic Defense class," Sabrina noted with excitement.

Fred and Sabrina eventually made it to the Academy entrance and headed outside, where they were greeted by Amaris, Aureum, Fern, and the boy that Fred assumed to be Sage. They all stood by the big golden gates that surrounded the Academy and separated it from the rest of the Sorcerer Realm.

"Sabrina!" Aureum exclaimed as she tackled Fred's daughter with a tight hug. "I'm going to miss you so much!" Sabrina laughed awkwardly and patted her on the back. "I'll miss you too, Aureum."

"Chirp!"

Fred jumped at the sudden sound of a chicken. He then noticed a baby chick with horns on its head on the ground beside Aureum.

Sabrina laughed and crouched down to pet the little chick, much to everyone else's confusion. "I'll miss you too, Chi," Sabrina said before being hugged by Fern, who looked like she was trying hard not to cry.

"Gosh, I'm going to miss having a roommate! You better come back and visit, ya hear me?" Fern warned, trying to be intimidating.

Sabrina stifled a laugh. "I hear you," she assures her.

Fern raised an eyebrow. "You'd better."

The two girls hugged again. It made Fred glad to know that Sabrina had good friends who cared about her as much as he did.

Sabrina smiled sadly as she adjusted her backpack on her back and exhaled.

"You know, it kind of sucks and doesn't make any sense, but I only got to spend one full day here. I only had one full day of knowing that I could use magic. I didn't even get to learn how to use it properly and poof—it's gone," she grumbled in annoyance.

Everyone looked at Sabrina with sympathy, and she scrunched up her nose.

"Hey, don't look at me like that! Don't pity me! Is one not allowed to complain without being pitied?" She asked, and everyone mumbled some incoherent reply.

"Are you ready to go, Dad?" Sabrina asked, glancing at Fred.

"As ready as I'll ever be. Thank you again, Amaris, for letting us return. I know it must be hard for you, because it's forbidden and you don't like to bend the rules, but I truly appreciate it."

Amaris sighed. "Please don't bring it up. I'm only doing this for the benefit of the future. Oh, and Sabrina? Sage is here because he wanted to say goodbye. Also, we will be holding a ceremony to say goodbye to

Sylvester in the near future, so I assume you'll return for that?" Fred swallowed hard but nodded. "Wonderful. I'll expect to see you again, then." Amaris offered Sabrina a small smile. Sabrina forced one in return.

"Hey, Sabrina, wait," Sage called to Sabrina.

"Yeah?" Sabrina answered.

"Be safe," he murmured.

Fred noticed Sabrina's frown, but she quickly covered up her confusion and nodded. Sabrina seemed to be confused as to why this Sage boy was concerned for her safety, as was Fred, but neither of them questioned it. "Um, yeah. I will," Sabrina assured him, and Sage flashed a smile with a nod.

"Shall we get going, Sabrina?" Fred asked, making his way to stand beside his daughter.

Sabrina gave him a lopsided smile as she held out her arm to Fred, and Fred took it. "Wait," Sabrina said sheepishly as she glanced down at the ring on her finger.

"What is it, Sabrina?" Fred asked with worry.

"I, uh, have no idea as to how to use this. Angelica just kind of gave it to me," Sabrina admitted awkwardly.

"Allow me," Amaris said as she walked toward the two.

Sabrina showed Amaris her hand, and Amaris studied the ring.

Then her eyes brightened as she seemed to realize how to use it.

"Of course! How could I have forgotten? Just think of what realm you wish to go to and where in the realm you want to be. Then press down on the gem on the ring," Amaris instructed as she released Sabrina's hand.

Sabrina nodded. "Okay. Sounds easy enough."

"I wish you both the best of luck. Frederick, keep me updated, all right? We can work on ways to track down and defeat Caspian. Just because Sabrina is now powerless, that does not mean that all hope is lost. Where there is a will, there's a way," Amaris said.

"Of course. I'll do everything within my power to keep in touch with you. Not to mention that Sabrina and I will be returning shortly to say a farewell to Sylvester," Fred said carefully. He then sighed and glanced at Sabrina. "Let's go," he said with a small smile.

Sabrina faintly smiles back, and Fred gently grabbed her arm again.

"Good luck, Sabrina!" Fern exclaimed.

"Don't get killed!" Aureum chimed in.

Sabrina laughs as she brushed a stray piece of her hair behind her ear. "I'll do my best," she replied before following Amaris's instructions.

She pressed down on the center of the ring with her eyes closed.

Fred decided that it must have worked, because the next thing he knew, everything was spinning and his vision went temporarily black.

XII. "Angelica Henry's Gift"

Sabrina prayed that the ring had worked and was assured that it did when her fluttered open. She felt drained, as she did every time that she'd realm traveled. She groaned as she rubbed her eyes, trying to wake herself up and get her senses to kick in. Her vision slowly came into focus, and she rolled over onto her back, feeling a familiar cushion beneath her. It was almost like she was back home and on her bed.

Bed! That's it!

Sabrina shot up into a sitting position, ignoring the pain that she felt in her stomach. She looked around and found herself back home, in her bedroom. She was lying on her bed, still in her clothes that she had changed into before she and her Dad had left.

Dad!

This got Sabrina moving.

Sabrina pushed her bed covers aside and went to run out the door when her foot suddenly hit something hard, causing her to lose her balance and trip. Sabrina grunted as she forced herself to sit up and see what she had tripped over.

It was her sword that she had summoned while battling Caspian.

Sabrina frowned as she picked it up, studying the blade. Sabrina didn't know how the sword had gotten here. She hadn't thought much of the sword after she'd woken up at the Academy.

She now wondered what had happened to it in all of the chaos.

How did it get into her room?

Sabrina then noticed a sticky note on the tip of the sword, and peeled it off. On the sticky was a note from Angelica, which confused Sabrina even more.

Dear Sabrina Banner,

Keep this sword and use it for protection. Only you can summon this sword. If you want it to disappear, then look at it and think that. If you wish for it to reappear, imagine it in your hand. Use the sword wisely. Please take care of yourself, and think before you act.

Best Wishes,
Angelica Henry

Sabrina hummed aloud in thought, trying to figure out how Angelica got the sword here. Angelica was dead, after all.

Sabrina finally sighed in defeat, knowing that she would most likely never learn the answer. She looked at the sword in her grasp, closed her eyes, and imagined it disappearing. As Angelica said it would, it disappeared.

Sabrina hoped that it would reappear like Angelica had claimed it would. She let out a deep breath, knowing that she had spent too much time in her room and needed to find out what everyone else was up to.

She needed to know how Aunt Jeanette had handled her dad, how Paris reacted, and what Demi and Jason were doing.

With a plan in mind, Sabrina set it into motion as she exited her bedroom, slowly descended the staircase, and waited to see whether anyone was talking downstairs.

Then as if on cue, she heard Demi say, "Where is Sabrina? It's been four days, and she hasn't texted either of us once! We made plans, y'know."

"Yeah! And if she wanted to cancel, or if the plans changed, she would've texted us at the very least!" Sabrina heard Jason add.

"Look, Sabrina wasn't feeling well. She's upstairs resting. I told her to stay off of her phone and get some sleep," Aunt Jeanette tried to reason with Sabrina's friends, but Sabrina knew that those two wouldn't back down. They were stubborn and wouldn't believe Aunt Jeanette that easily unless they could see Sabrina for themselves. It was something to love and hate about them, in Sabrina's opinion.

"How can that be possible? Sabrina hardly ever gets sick! And then you also claim for this weirdo to be her long lost father when we all know that her dad and mom died when she was a child!" Demi said.

Sabrina chewed on the inside of her cheek in thought, feeling slightly stressed and anxious. She needed to think of something, and fast.

Something that would make sense and wouldn't make Demi and Jason think she was lying. Sabrina couldn't leave her aunt and dad at the mercy of her friends, who would find the answers they were looking for no matter the cost.

"I really am Sabrina's father," Fred remarked.

Demi scoffed, not believing it. "Yeah, right."

Sabrina exhaled loudly, letting her shoulders slump with defeat. She would have to go in there and face her friends.

"Just let us see her. Then we'll leave, I promise! I'm just worried about her," Demi cried.

Aunt Jeanette replied, "Demi, I'm sorry, but I don't want her spreading her sickness to—"

Sabrina decided to take this as her cue to interrupt. Mustering up courage and putting a smile onto her face, Sabrina walked into the living room with pride.

"Sea!" Demi squealed happily, and she ran over to hug Sabrina.

"Sabrina!" the others family said with equal delight.

Sabrina laughed and smiled at her family. Everyone was there: Paris, Aunt Jeanette, Demi, Jason … and her dad.

"You're not dead *or* sick! Ha! I knew it!" Demi screeched victoriously as she squeezed Sabrina tightly in their hug.

"Um, Demi, I can't breathe!" Sabrina wheezed, trying to pry her best friend off of her. She had already been almost choked to death once. There was no need to make it twice.

Demi blushed and quickly released Sabrina.

"Oh, sorry!"

Sabrina waves her hand in dismissal. "It's fine. But it does feel good to breathe like a normal person," Sabrina joked, and Demi gave her a sheepish smile. "Hey, Jase."

He was patiently waiting, unlike Demi.

"Hey, Sabrina," Jason said, and they hugged each other.

"Okay, so I know I have some explaining to do," Sabrina began nervously after Jason and Sabrina pulled apart from their hug.

"Yeah, you do! Like, what's up with the cut on your lip?" Paris asked as she rushed over to Sabrina and held Sabrina's face in her hand.

Sabrina frowned, confused as to what Paris was talking about.

"What cut? Oh, right. Well, um, I accidentally hit my lip on … on my nightstand. Yeah! It's a long story, actually, so I'm not going to go into any detail, but I'm fine, really."

Paris looked like she was trying to resist the urge to tackle Sabrina with a bone-crushing hug, and Sabrina appreciates Paris for not doing that. Sabrina's hand suddenly traveled to the dead phone in her pocket. She fingered it and shifted uncomfortably on her feet.

Then she closed her eyes, calming herself.

She knew she'd have to lie because mortals couldn't know about the Sorcerer Realm.

Well, they can know about it, but they can't think it's real.

To them it's just a myth.

And that's how it has to stay.

Sabrina reopened her eyes, let out a shaky breath, and knew it was now or never. If she hesitated any longer, they would become suspicious and less easy to fool.

"Sabrina, are you okay?" Paris asked Sabrina, concern evident in her voice.

Sabrina forced a hopefully convincing smile onto her face and nodded.

"Yeah, Paris. I'm fine, really. But anyway, Jason and Demi, I'm so sorry about not texting you guys. My phone was acting up, and a lot has gone down in the past few days. For starters, Aunt Jeanette wasn't lying when she said I've been sick. It's true. I'm just now getting over it." Sabrina lies right through her teeth.

"Also, this guy really is my dad. Apparently something happened that caused him and my mom to have to separate. His job forced him to move away, and he didn't want my Mom to have to move as well. So without thinking, he left her a note and left. He felt bad, of course, but he didn't want to make things harder on her and me. Now he's come back after reconnecting with Aunt Jeanette and apologizing for everything."

Demi and Jason shared a look before Demi turned her head and analyzed Sabrina's dad, narrowing her eyes in the process.

"Okay, Sabrina. We believe you. But you did get police to confirm this stuff, right? Because he could still be lying ..." Demi shifted her gaze from Sabrina's dad to Sabrina.

Sabrina nodded. "Yeah, we did. We did a blood test and everything. He's my dad, and it's in his and my record."

"All right, fine. But don't say I didn't warn you if he turns out to be not who he seems!"

"Relax, Demi. I trust him, and so does Aunt Jeanette and Paris," Sabrina claimed, hoping that Paris or Aunt Jeanette wouldn't interject. Fortunately, they didn't.

"Okay. But if you need anything, you know who to call," Demi concluded.

Sabrina sighed. "Yes, Demi. I'll keep that in mind."

"Well I have to get going," Jason said, glancing over at Demi. "I don't know about you, but I've got homework to finish up before spring break ends."

Sabrina's face fell.

Oh, right.

Homework.

That's a thing.

She mentally cursed herself for forgetting about her homework.

When you're living a double life and are off saving all of the realms, you kind of forget that you've got a normal life to keep track of as well.

"Ha! Sucks for you, Jase! I got my homework done on the first day of spring break," Demi gloated.

Jason rolled his eyes. "What a little overachiever you are," he teased.

"Yep!" Demi beamed, not getting that Jason was mocking her.

Sabrina chuckled at their antics.

They were always teasing and picking on each other like that.

"But I *am* supposed to watch my little sister for my parents soon, so I should be going as well. Make sure you text us, Sabrina, once you get your phone fixed," Demi said.

Sabrina smiled and gave her best friend a clumsy captain's salute. "Will do!" She and her friends laughed.

"See you at school, Sabrina. And you too, Paris. Also, have a good night Mrs. Banner, and it's nice to meet you, uh ..." Jason began as he looked at Sabrina's dad, not knowing what to say.

"Please, call me, Fred," Sabrina's dad said.

"Okay. It was nice to meet you, Fred," Jason said, testing it out.

"Come on, Jase. Let's get going. Bye, guys!" Demi said as she headed out the door.

"Bye!" Sabrina and her family replied as Jason and Demi head out.

Sabrina sighed when the door closed. She leaned against the wall, feeling exhausted.

"Nice cover-up," Fred complimented.

Sabrina shrugged. "It was the best thing I could think of on such short notice."

"Well, it worked."

"Okay, okay. Now that Demi and Jason are gone, spill!" Paris said, no longer able to contain her curiosity.

"And what really happened to your lip, Sabrina?" Fred asked, knowing full well that his daughter had the cut on her lip before they came here. Aunt Jeanette nodded in agreement.

Sabrina sighed again before replying. "I suppose that we should sit down. It's going to be a long story."

The four of them headed to the living room, where they made themselves comfortable and sat down, ready to listen to Sabrina's story.

Sabrina explained everything that had happened since she'd left the Mortal Realm. She talked about how she'd met Sylvester, Fern, and Aureum. She discussed her first, and probably last, time taking lessons at the Academy.

She recalled Sylvester, Aureum, and her sneaking out of the Academy, as well as the bus accident. She told them about staying in the motel, but she left out the part about Sylvester using dark magic.

Eventually she got to the part where the nightshades tracked them down and knocked them out, taking them as prisoners to Caspian's hideout.

Then Sabrina retold what she could remember of her battle with Caspian, Caspian killing her, Sabrina summoning the Sword of a Half-Blood, and Sabrina meeting Angelica and getting her RTD before waking up at the Academy. Everyone listened intently, intrigued in one way or another about her adventure.

"So … that's what happened," Sabrina concluded.

Paris surprised Sabrina by giving her a big, bone-crushing hug and saying, "I'm glad that you're okay. And no more dying, all right? Most people are fortunate enough to have one chance at life. You got two. Don't waste your second chance."

Sabrina nodded. "I have no intentions of wasting it."

Paris smiles and ruffles Sabrina's hair, much to Sabrina's discontent. "It's good to have you back, little cousin. And it's nice to meet you, Uncle Fred," Paris remarked, looking at Sabrina and then at Fred, who smiles at his niece.

"Same here, Paris," Fred replied, and Sabrina nodded in agreement.

"Well, Fred, how about I take you to my bakery?" Aunt Jeanette offered with a warm smile. "We've only met once, so we have much to catch up on if you're going to be staying with me and my daughter for a while. And girls, you're welcome to come along."

"Thank you, Aunt Jeanette, but we have school tomorrow, and I have a lot of homework to do," Sabrina politely excused herself.

Aunt Jeanette smiled and kissed Sabrina on the forehead in a motherly way. "No worries, Sabrina. I'll bring you back something to eat for later." Sabrina continued smiling. "Paris, are you coming?"

"Yeah, definitely!" Paris grinned as she ran to catch up with them.

"Wonderful! We'll be back soon, Sabrina," Aunt Jeanette called out as she put on her coat and reached for the doorknob.

"Stay out of trouble, Sabrina," Fred joked.

"What makes you think that I'd get into trouble?" Sabrina replied with a cheeky grin.

Fred laughed and shook his head. "No reason. No reason at all."

The trio headed out the door, leaving Sabrina by herself.

Sabrina soon finds herself laying on her bed and let out a sigh of exhaustion after finishing all of her homework. She turned her head and stared out her window, where the sun was beginning to set. Her mind wanders off as her inner dialogue took over.

People say when door closes, another one opens, or that not everything is as it seems. Sabrina used to not believe that. Then she met Sylvester. In her short life, Sabrina had had multiple doors close and new ones open that she'd never dared to go through. Sabrina had tried different paths to try to find who she was supposed to be.

She still hadn't found herself, but she knew that after this adventure, Sabrina was only a puzzle piece closer to finding the last piece.

The road ahead of her will be risky.

Sabrina knew that now. She also knew that she was not normal.

She had never been. Her life was no longer boring or ordinary either. In fact, now it is the exact opposite.

She had simply been too blind to see what it was about her that made her special.

Now that Sabrina knew, there's no going back. Sabrina had been betrayed by the one she had thought to be her friend.

She had learned of a different world that no mortal had ever known. She no longer felt cheated by being born in the wrong time period.

Sabrina used to think that everything had been discovered, but now she knew that wasn't case. Things were going to get messy, and she was well aware of that.

Sabrina was probably going to lose people whom she held dear. Caspian was going to stop at nothing to win.

But what else would be expected of him?

That meant Sabrina had to be just as determined, and that was what she planned to do. The battle wasn't over yet—this was simply the beginning. Sabrina had a lot more to uncover and a lot more that needed to be done if she planned on surviving.

Sabrina stared up at the ceiling and sighed as she twirled her new ring around her finger.

"Just face it, Sabrina. You're screwed. The whole world is going to die, and it'll be your fault. There's no walking around that," she mumbled before closing her eyes and letting sleep take its toll on her.

Whoever decided to put the fate of the realms and universe into the hands on an anxious and slightly insecure teenage girl must've been completely out of their mind.